TEMPLAR SCROLLS

THE NIA RIVERS ADVENTURES BOOK 3

INES JOHNSON

THOSE JOHNSON GIRLS

Through the ages of my long life, one truth always remained. It was the one fact that had never failed me. And that truth was there was nothing a little salt water couldn't cure.

I'd crossed the Pacific Ocean and made it to the West Coast of the New World before Columbus's boat had even been built. Four hundred years later, I'd survived the sinking of the Titanic in the Atlantic Ocean. Just a few years ago, I'd evaded Somali pirates in the Arabian Sea after taking samples of Dhambalin art, which depicted ancient drawings of cattle and sheep dated more than five thousand years old.

Throughout all these sea adventures, the curative properties of salt water reigned true. It cleansed the colon, releasing toxins accumulated in the digestive tract. It was great for skin care, clearing pores and combating acne. Sprinkle a little salt on a bland dish and everyone's taste buds would water. Sea waters washed away waste, blemishes, stains, sweat, and tears.

All throughout my past, whenever something ailed me, I ran to the sea. These waters, rough one day, calm the next, were no place for the weak. The rolling ocean of blue required patience, cunning, and steadfastness to navigate. The sea stretched out to give me room to breathe, surrounding me and smothering me with attention at the same time. Its tranquility embraced me, wrapped me up in lulling waves, and allowed me to see my next course of action.

Not going to the waters after my initial heartbreak had been a mistake. I'd been left battered and bruised by love this year. But now, the sea air was healing my aches and pains.

I'd been sailing for over a week after leaving Greece with my best friend Loren, also known as the girlfriend most likely to key her ex's car with a sword. She and I had emerged largely unscathed from the battle of the Greek gods and their twisted version of familial love. That demigod drama was now behind us, and I was finally starting to feel a bit better.

When we'd left the Mediterranean Sea, it had been mostly calm and placid. The horizon had been clear. The Meltemi winds, which often lashed out from land and caused mischief in the waters, had left Loren and me alone. It was once we got into the Celtic Sea that the tides began to turn, as often happened when leaving a tropical clime for a cold and damp one. The storm had come out of nowhere like the flu on the first day of summer.

Like the tickle that began in the back of the throat, the waters began tugging at the boat's anchor. In the same way that the flu virus would spread from the throat through the neck, the ripples of the waters sent the boat rocking to and fro. Like in a head cold when the sickness would fog the brain, the foam of the whitecaps broke at the bow of the boat, sending a spray that misted our eyes and temporarily blurred our vision. The waves bunched about the ship like the restless fingers of nausea. The stern groaned a dry heave as though the heart of the ship was about to break.

I gripped the steering wheel as the waves broke all around me, rising, falling, and thrashing my vessel. The storm felt like it required superhuman strength to navigate. Luckily, I was superhuman. Not only that, but I also had the skill and endurance to make my way through the tempest.

"I feel like we're up a creek without a paddle," said Loren. "Only the creek is an ocean and there are no paddles on yachts. Are there?"

The humor in her voice was strained. Her fingers curled tight around the railing. Her knuckles turned white at the force of her grip. A tremor wobbled her knees as another wave broke and battered the side of the boat.

"Loren, go below deck and make sure everything is secure."

Everything was already secure. My preparations were impeccable, as always. I took pride in any vessel I commanded. I knew the boat was secure; I just wanted my bestie out of harm's way.

Loren ignored my command and stayed by my side. "Someone needs to watch your back."

It wasn't my back I was worried about. I could weather this storm, but her human body wouldn't heal if it was thrown overboard. I'd paid attention to the weather forecast. Nothing about the fast winds of this storm had been predicted. Gale winds were manageable in this day and time because there were normally forewarnings well in advance of the winds' arrival upon a boat.

I didn't need to rely on any predictions. I'd been sailing for hundreds of years. I knew how to read the clouds. The cyclonic system followed a predictable sequence. Each cycle had its own cloud formation, wind shift, and weather pattern. Nothing in the movements of the sky could have predicted what was going on in these waters.

We'd gotten further inland at the end of the Celtic Sea as we neared the British Isles. We weren't too far beyond the continental shelf, that area of seabed around a large landmass. Since it was relatively shallow as compared to the open sea, I was considering deploying the sea anchor.

I'd turned off the self-steering system and was helming the yacht by hand, which was tiring, especially at night. I might be strong and Immortal, but I needed a break before I made a mistake that could cost my friend her life.

I was considering finding shelter in a sea inlet, a loch. Often in those narrow pockets, the weather was different, like standing in the eye of a hurricane. I just had to get us to one.

But for the second time today, just as soon as the storm had come, the winds died down. The waters calmed. It felt supernatural. For a moment, I wondered if it was the Greek god Poseidon messing around with me.

He'd played around with me before, pulling practical jokes that made me think I was seeing things in the water when I'd journeyed into Greece last month. But we'd left him behind a couple of weeks ago in Athens. I didn't get the impression that the seal-hugging environmentalist got his kicks out of dashing a vessel around with two women on board. The middle brother of the Olympian clan was too laid back, cool, and collected for this.

"What happened?" Loren asked. Her voice echoed into the eerie silence that had settled over us like a warm blanket on a winter's night.

"I don't know."

I put the boat back on self-steering and slumped into a deck chair. After running shaky fingers over my brow, I clutched at my stomach, feeling a touch of sea sickness for the first time in my long life. My body and brain were exhausted.

Loren slid down into a chair beside me. "I saw my life flash before my eyes."

Thankfully, I hadn't seen mine. Who knew how long that would've taken. I had no idea how old I was. But I'd been around long enough that the reel of my life would need to be played out over several showings in a day. Possibly a week.

"I heard my mom calling out my name," Loren continued.

I turned to study her. Her blonde tresses looked as though they hadn't seen a brush in a week. Light blue eyes were glassy and dazed. Her chest caved in as she wrapped her arms around herself.

Loren and I had only known each other for about three months. Her father and I had been in the same line of work—archaeology. But Dr. Van Alst and I had never met in person. I had met a handful of Loren's lovers, and she'd met two of mine. But we'd never discussed her mother. Or where Loren lived in her normal, non-adventurous life. Or if she had left something behind to come gallivanting around the world with me. I realized I knew so little about this person I'd spent nearly every day with for the last quarter of a year.

"You've never told me about your mother," I said.

Loren shrugged. "She died when I was very young. She was from England, some tiny little town in Somerset called Glastonbury. I've never been."

I had. I'd visited it a couple of hundred years ago when it was still called Glistening Town because of the witches and wizards who'd lived there.

"I don't remember much about her," Loren continued. "Her name was Magda. Can you imagine?" She shuddered as though the Germanic name tasted sickly-sweet on her tongue.

It wasn't an uncommon name. Well, maybe a couple of hundred years ago it was.

"She was blonde with blue eyes that sparkled," Loren said. Her mouth settled into a small smile after swallowing the bitterness of her mother's name. "At least that's how I remember them as a child. I remember the sound of her voice. It sounded like a piccolo, one of those tiny little flutes. Light and happy. It made me want to dance and hold still and listen all at once."

I stared at her. This was the first time I'd ever heard Loren wax philosophical. Normally, she had a biting wit, a sharp tongue, and a twinkle of mischief in her eyes.

"It sounds like you remember her pretty well," I said.

"No." Loren shook her head, frowning now. "I don't know anything else about her, except that very short list. My father didn't like to talk about her. I remember he was devastated after she died. Like the unable-to-pull-himself-out-of-bed type of devastated. He never looked at another woman again. I think that's why I cringe at relationships. The idea that someone could have such a massive effect on your life…it's terrifying."

I understood. Even now, with the salt in the air and the sea waters sprinkling my face, I still felt the pangs in my heart. I didn't know if I could ever let another man get as close to me as I had let Zane. And he was very much alive. But the disentanglement process felt like murder inside my body.

"I do remember her reading to me," Loren said. "She loved the tales of Arthur and his Knights of the Round Table. I remember lying in my bed, which was usually a cot in a tent because we traveled with my father most of the time. She'd read me the tales of Lancelot and Guinevere, Sir Gawain, and the Green Knight he had to battle to the death. Tristan and Isolde and their star-crossed love. Sir Galahad and his quest for the Holy Grail was my favorite. I loved those stories. They probably screwed me up, though, making me believe a man would come and rescue me. Like that would ever happen in modern times."

Loren and I were far from damsels. We carried blades on our hips and knew how to use them. The weapons were often accessorized with designer purses slung over vintage tops. A woman should look her best while she was kicking butt.

"Now I get to meet the real Arthur." Loren's gaze twinkled with a mix of delight and mischief.

"Not the actual Arthur. He died over a thousand years ago. This is his..." I had to count the Arthurs in my head as well as on my fingers. "Great-grandson."

"That's only four generations."

"Yeah," I agreed.

"So this Arthur has to be at least a couple of hundred years old?"

I nodded. "They age really well in Camelot."

"How?" Loren said. "Are they Immortal, too?"

"No. They're something else. You wouldn't believe me if I told you."

"So far, I've seen ninjas flying over my head, Greek gods shooting lightning bolts, and humans getting their souls sucked out of their eyes, so not sure there is much I *wouldn't* consider believing anymore."

She had seen all those things. And in each of those adventures, she'd nearly lost her life standing by my side, just like she almost had during the storm. Guilt swept over me. One of these days I was probably going to get her killed.

My life was dangerous for someone supernatural. It was disastrous for a mortal. That was the reason why I didn't allow myself to get too attached to humans. They were fragile creatures, easily breakable in body, mind, and spirit. I hadn't tried to send Loren away, but I knew one day she'd leave me on her own or die trying.

"We're getting close," I said.

We were headed to Caerleon in the south of Great Britain. The Arthur had requested my presence for something to do with the Holy Grail. It was purported to be the cup the prophet Jesus used at the Last Supper. But it was also rumored to be the cup into which his blood fell during his crucifixion. Men had fought and died to find and possess the cup, believing it held magical powers. But from what I knew, it had been safe in the Knights of the Round Table's possession for hundreds of years. Their castle, Tintagel, was an impenetrable fortress, even for someone like me.

When an emissary brought an invitation for me to cross the drawbridge a couple of weeks ago, I'd jumped at the chance. Not too high, though. I didn't want The Arthur to know how eager I was to storm his castle. There were more ancient artifacts behind the walls than just the drinking cup, and I wanted to get my hands on them—just to look, of course. But I needed to get there first.

However, the closer we drew to the British Isles, the more the winds picked up. It was as though something was trying to keep us from the shore.

Out on the horizon, I spotted another boat. The seas churned it up and down like a roller coaster. The other vessel sent up a distress signal. The waves crested, and I saw two bodies pulled off the ship and dropped into the unforgiving waters. No human would survive such a fall, much less be able to swim through those waves.

I made a rash decision. I dropped the anchor.

"Loren, stay here."

For once, I hoped she'd listen to me. I dove into the waters and headed for the ship in distress.

CHAPTER TWO

The impact stung my cheeks, and the salt burned my eyes. I swam fast and furiously in my attempts to reach the distressed boat. At my speed, I could keep up with a sailfish, one of the fastest fish in the oceans. My body moved easily through the water's depths. I broke the surface to see I was more than halfway to the other vessel. Wiping the water from my eyes, I still had to blink a couple of times because I couldn't believe what I saw.

It was difficult to sink a ship. After all, the vessels were designed to stay afloat, unlike submarines that rose and sank. It was common for waves to break over the sides of a ship and for tiny leaks to occur. But those rivulets of water would eventually find their way to the lowest point of the boat, the bilge, where the small stream would be pumped out. The waves crashing into this ship looked as though they were reaching up from the bowels of the sea and actively pulling it down into its depths.

I'd never seen anything like it. It was like a freak storm from hell—if hell were in the oceans. The scene looked like the boat had been caught in an Oz-like tornado swirling it around and lifting it out of Kansas. It crashed into the water, causing a mighty splash that pulled me under.

I saw two bodies beneath the surface. The bodies looked as though they were suspended in motion as they sank into the murky deep. I set into action, diving to reach them, hoping to get to them before all the air left their lungs.

As I got nearer, something flashed before my eyes. It looked as though it had been a pair of fins. But the scales were white and flowed out, almost like it could've been a fan's tail. Or a nightgown. I swore I saw hair as white as strands of moonlight, but I blinked and the vision was gone.

I knew of only one being who could live beneath the surfaces of the ocean. And he had brown skin and dark locks. There were no such things as mermaids. At least I didn't remember ever meeting any.

There were humans who could shift their shapes. But that tribe of people shifted into land mammals, reptiles, and birds. And they were all in the Americas.

The storm raged on above me. I turned my attention back to the people who'd fallen from the sinking ship. I raced to them, kicking my legs powerfully, shoving the water out of my way with my arms until I reached them.

Neither man appeared to kick, flail, or fight for his life. Their arms were stretched above them, as though hoping for the guiding hand of a god or an angel.

I wrapped my arm around the first man. In the water, bodies weighed less, so I was able to maneuver him in one arm while I used my other to steer me toward his companion.

Reaching the second man, I grabbed his limp body. It was difficult to propel forward without the use of my arms, but I managed. I was strong enough to heft them through the waters and get them back to my ship. Superhuman, remember.

It took me twice as long to make it back with my human cargo. The storm continued to wail and groan behind me as it focused its attack on the abandoned ship and left mine in relative peace.

With Loren's help, I hefted the two bodies onto the deck.

One man wore the dark blue and gold braids of a captain. The other wore a simple white shirt and slacks. He could've been a passenger or one of the captain's mates. There was no way for me to tell. The captain had a gash across his forehead. His mate looked as though his arm might be broken. The limb rested at an odd angle.

Loren began CPR on the mate while I started compressions on the captain. The mate coughed up water and then immediately howled in pain, grasping at his twisted arm. He went silent when he saw me working on the captain. The mate clutched at his arm and gritted his teeth. He looked as though he was holding his breath as we all waited for the captain to take a breath of his own.

Finally, the older man gasped and then coughed up the sea. I turned him on his side to help get the salt water out of his airway. A shiver went through his body as he shifted onto his back. His eyes were unfocused, but the one word he uttered was clear.

"Father?" said the captain. His head turned back in the direction of his failing vessel, and his hand reached out.

The man beside the captain looked too young to

be his father. I turned back to the sinking ship. I hadn't seen another body in the water. Was someone else still trapped on the distressed boat?

The waters continued to batter the sides of the ship. The vessel looked like it had sunk lower on the horizon. It was only a matter of time before the sea swallowed it whole. There wasn't time to debate. I stood at the side of my boat and dove back into the water to save the captain's father.

In the depths, it was silent and peaceful. The moon's light broke through the water to shine in the darkness. The water that flowed past my ears was a silent symphony of calm. But when I broke the surface, the gale winds came from every direction, battering the ship. In hundreds of years of sailing the open waters and coastal areas, I'd never seen an isolated storm such as this. I peered over my shoulder and saw my yacht was in relatively calm waters in comparison.

The other ship had sunk low enough that it was no trouble climbing aboard. When I did, the waters that had cradled me on my way here turned abusive. The ripples lashed out at me from every direction. The waters washed anything not bolted overboard and into the churning waters.

Sandwiched in a corner, I found a man. When I

got to him, I noted he looked young, much younger than the captain. If this man had any children, they couldn't be more than toddlers, even if he'd started very young. Was someone else still on board? Then I saw the priest collar gripped in his hand. So, not a biological father but a spiritual one.

The man had passed out. He was unresponsive but alive. I put him over my back and dove into the waters just in time. The ship groaned as the waves claimed it.

In the waters, I saw that flash of white again, like sheer cloth that would cover a woman's legs as she reposed. But instead of feet, I saw a blinding light. It knocked me back, pulling me under.

It felt as though something was tethered around my foot, yanking me down to the seafloor. The force was strong. I was stronger, but I was also tired. Still, I knew I had to fight.

I could hold my breath underwater for an inhumanly long time. But the man I carried couldn't. I kicked for the surface and finally broke through, feeling the heartbeat of the man on my back. It was weak, but it was there.

As I made my way to my boat, I noticed that the winds had stopped. The waves were calming. An eerie stillness settled over the water. A glance over my shoulder showed me that the other boat was sinking faster now. In just a matter of minutes it would be gone, as though it had never been there at all.

It had taken the Titanic nearly three hours to sink. I knew. I'd watched it go down as people around me shivered and others sank to their deaths. The boat before me was nowhere near the size of that doomed vessel. It also hadn't split in two. But it sank as though it had been broken into a million tiny pieces. It also sank straight down, not tilting up or to the side like a normal sinking vessel.

I couldn't stare and wonder at the marvel any longer. For the third time tonight, I had a non-responsive man mounted on my back, which wasn't doing much for my feminine ego. I was so exhausted that my tired was tired by the time I got myself and my quarry back on board my boat.

"Oh," Loren said, placing a dramatic hand to her chest as her eyebrows rose. "Look what the storm dragged in." She gave the man a coquettish look that would have been funny had he been awake.

With the third man laid out on the deck, I could see what she was fussing about. This guy was handsome. He reminded me of that tall actor with the deep Texas drawl, Matthew McConaughey. This man had the same dirty-blond hair. His limbs were long and muscled, his chin square, and his cheekbones high. His lips were blue at the moment, but their shape hinted that they could be set in a serious line or pulled up in a sensual grin.

He'd lost his collar somewhere in the waters. I didn't bother warning Loren off. He was unconscious. There was nothing she could do—at least, I didn't think so.

I assumed I would have to fight her over who would get to give him mouth-to-mouth resuscitation, but before I could even begin compressions, his eyes opened. He coughed up sea water. And when his lungs were empty, his eyes fastened onto Loren. They were blue, by the way. I would've sworn this guy was the Hollywood actor... until he began to speak.

"Are you an angel?" he drawled, but his accent wasn't southern. At least not from the southern part of the United States. He was Italian. Maybe the south of Italy.

Loren sighed. I did, too. But they were two entirely different sounds.

Part of the reason Loren and I were out sailing was to get over our past relationships. Loren was anti-relationship as a rule. She'd been betrayed by the only guy she'd dated more than once. I had recently broken up with my boyfriend of five hundred years and then started dating a guy I'd dated a thousand years ago. But a couple of weeks ago, I'd fallen back into bed with my ex. I'd come to the sea hoping to find myself, but I was still wallowing in confusion. Loren was already on to the next guy.

"Welcome to heaven," she said.

"I am delivered." He reached out to her. His fingers hovered just before her face, as though he dared not touch a celestial being.

"Father Gerard?" said the captain.

Loren's face contorted as she looked between the two men. The captain was clearly the elder of the two.

"Father?" Loren said.

Father Gerard sat up, wincing as he did so.

I reached to check his body in an attempt to find any blood or broken bones. "Careful," I warned, even as I didn't find anything amiss on his person. It was miraculous he'd survived at all. But survived with his body intact? That was supernatural.

"The boat?" Father Gerard asked, trying to look out on the horizon.

"It's gone down," I confirmed.

Father Gerard looked around, as though to count his shipmates.

"We're all here," the captain confirmed.

His shipmate sat beside him with his arm in a makeshift brace courtesy of Loren.

"It is by the grace of God we are still on this earth," said the captain in a shaky voice, his eyes still wide from their ordeal.

No, it was by the grace of me. But as always for my great feats, I didn't get any credit.

The priest stood on weak legs and looked out at the sinking ship. Nothing remained of the vessel. The waters and wind had calmed now that the ship had gone down.

"Lord, have mercy," muttered the man of God. Father Gerard turned back to Loren and me, assessing us. "How did you save us?"

"Oh..." I said. "We just fished you out of the water. No big deal."

"We owe you our lives." The priest's voice was fervent. His attention remained on Loren. "You must be our guardian angel."

I tugged at my soaked top. My lips pressed into a mute slash. I decided to not be jealous as the credit went elsewhere.

"I've never seen a storm like that," the captain

said. "Been sailing these waters all my life." Unlike Father Gerard, the captain sounded as though he was a Welshman.

"Where were you all headed?" I asked.

"Shropshire," Father Gerard answered.

"We're headed near there. We'll radio the Coast Guard about your boat and get you guys to land."

"Thank you," he said. Again, to Loren and not me.

"We should probably get you out of those wet clothes," Loren said suggestively as she guided him below deck.

I sighed. She was incorrigible.

"*L*oren, you can't flirt with a priest."

"I've never seen that written in the Bible."

I sighed again as I steered the ship. I'd been doing that a lot—the sighing, I meant. I didn't know which surprised me more—her words or that she might've actually read the Bible. Sailing was smooth now. The storm was gone, and we were getting nearer to land.

"He called me an angel," she said. "No man has ever called me that."

"He meant it biblically."

"I'd like to get to know him in the biblical way." She elbowed me in the ribs, laughing.

The man in question was walking about in a too-small terrycloth bathrobe as his clothes continued to dry out in the sun. It would seem he had no issues with modesty. He was certainly unlike any priest I'd ever met.

The captain and skipper were resting below deck recovering from their injuries. I'd patched up the captain's head. After examining the skipper's arm, I found it was only a mild sprain and not an actual break, but it needed support and rest.

"Feeling better?" Loren asked as Father Gerard came over and sat in one of the lounge-like deck chairs.

He kicked up his bare feet and rested his forearms on the chair arms. Leaning his head back, he smiled up at Loren.

"Feeling fantastic," he said. He sounded educated, but there was a hint of the streets on his tongue. "There's nothing like a near-death experience to get the blood pumping."

Loren sat next to him, giving him the side-eye. "Oh, I know a few things that could—"

"So, *Father*," I cut her off, emphasizing the man's occupation. "You were ordained by the Roman Catholic Church?"

"Uh..." He took a deep breath and then let out the next word in a gush of air. "No."

I blinked, waiting. He stared back, breathing easily now but not offering any other explanation.

"Oh," I said, putting the boat on self-steering to come and stand at the railing before him. "I just assumed, you know, since you're Italian."

He grinned. "Not all Italians are Catholics."

"I know that." Great. Now I sounded like a narrow-minded racist who had a prejudice against Catholics, which was far from the truth. I was uncomfortable around *any* humans who praised a deity, seen or unseen. "I just thought that because I saw you with the collar."

"My collar?" He touched his bare neck. Then he looked down to his hand, the one he'd been holding the collar in when I'd found him. But, like his neck, his hand was bare, empty. "I seemed to have lost it."

He took in another of those deep breaths. When he let this one out, it didn't come with any words. It just came with a half-hearted shrug.

"You've lost your faith?" Loren asked.

"Yes, I suppose I have." He looked up into the sky. "You would too if you'd seen the things I've seen."

His eyes took on a haunted sheen. His square jaw clenched. His lips pursed.

"Are you a soldier?" I asked.

Another deep breath through his nostrils. This time, he let out a soft chuckle. "That I am."

"War has lost many a man his faith," I said. I didn't ask which war he'd fought or ministered in. There was always more than one going on at any point in time of human history.

"Oh, no." He shook his head. "You misunderstand me. I haven't lost my faith in God." He spread his arms wide. "His glory is great indeed. Look at how he delivered me from the waves of death last night."

I sucked my teeth, but I didn't correct him. I didn't usually crave credit for my heroic acts. These were just three guys I'd happened upon and saved. I'd saved the entire country of Greece a couple of weeks ago, and had I asked for a parade? No. But a little thank you from a shipwreck survivor couldn't be too much to expect.

"Jesus Christ is now and will forever be my savior," Father Gerard continued.

I only nodded. I didn't let it be known I had known the man. He'd been called Yeshua in my time. He had also been called a prophet and a philosopher. It wasn't until his untimely death that his followers began calling him a savior.

By the time he was betrayed by his disciples, I

had already left and sailed across the oceans to the land that would one day become known as America. So, I wasn't sure if he actually rose from the grave. But the man I had known *had* been miraculous. Many of the miracles attributed to him had actually been true.

He was indeed a great healer. He was a heck of a fisherman. The water-into-wine thing, well, I had an explanation for that feat. I'd never gotten to ask him how he'd managed the walking-on-water bit. And, to this day, I still couldn't puzzle out how he'd done it.

Of course, I didn't tell Father Gerard this. Humans would get uncomfortable anytime I mentioned I had been on a first-name basis with their savior.

"It's my faith in man that I've lost," Father Gerard said, sounding tired. "I renounced my vows to the Church. I am only a humble servant of my God now. I keep his covenants over the laws of mankind."

I kept my smart mouth shut instead of asking him which covenant. There was the Noahic covenant where God promised never to destroy the world again and left the rainbow as the sign of this promise. There was the Abrahamic covenant that granted Abraham and a multitude of descendants a promised bit of land. There were the Mosaic covenants that included the Ten Commandments.

And there were others, but I remained mute. The man had been through an ordeal. A religious debate was the last thing he needed. But Loren didn't hold her tongue.

"So..." Loren said, drawing the word out. "That whole vow-of-celibacy thing?"

"Loren," I bit out.

She looked at me as though I was the one who had said something wrong.

Father Gerard only chuckled. "Though I no longer wear the collar, I do keep my priestly covenants. I maintain my vow of poverty, in that I own no property. My vow of obedience, in that I obey the laws of the one who commands my heart. And, yes, there is also a vow of chastity."

"Oh," Loren said, her lower lip pouting at the fact she wouldn't get any spirited activity today. But then she rallied, and her chest rose. At least she'd had the decency to put on a bra now that there were males onboard. "Wait, do you mean chastity in terms of pure of heart?"

"No." Father Gerard smiled. It wasn't a sad or sorrowful smile, and somehow his gaze managed a sensual reverence. "I am celibate."

"Of course you are." Loren's chest caved, and her shoulders slumped.

"Physical love is only one way to love," he offered.

"Yeah…" Loren sighed. "The best way."

"What were you all doing out at sea?" I asked, hoping to change the subject.

Father Gerard answered without tearing his gaze from Loren. "We sailed from Rome."

"Just a pleasure cruise?" I asked.

"Sadly, no."

I waited, but I had neither his attention nor any more of his words. He was still transfixed by Loren, whose wistful gaze was now on the horizon instead of the hunk.

"Business, then?" I asked.

"Hmm?" he said. "Oh, yes. I have some business to attend to in Shropshire."

"Why not fly into Manchester Airport? It's much quicker and safer."

"I like a bit of an adventure," he said.

"So do I," Loren said. "We just came from Greece after battling Greek gods. Now we're headed to England to help out some knights."

I glared at her for telling this stranger the truth. But the truth was far stranger than any fiction, and in response, Father Gerard only chuckled. Loren shrugged at me, as if to say no one would ever believe the stories we had to tell.

"I'm on a quest for knights as well," Father Gerard said.

"Really?" Loren asked. "To Camelot?"

My expression pinched as I glared at her. Loren had been thrust into a world where magic thrived. She didn't know all the rules. Mainly the first rule, which was *Don't talk about Supernatural Club.*

Father Gerard's eyes narrowed as his smile sharpened, like a shark's. My hackles went up at the abrupt change in his demeanor.

"You know of the Arthurian Legends?" he asked.

"My mother used to read them to me when I was a little girl." Loren had turned her body away from the celibate priest. She leaned back in now that he was talking about one of her favorite subjects. "But even back then, I questioned why there were no female knights. I'd begun handling a sword about the same time that I began to walk. I was better than any boy in my fencing classes. I've always thought I was born in the wrong time."

"If you were born in medieval times," I said, "you wouldn't have been allowed anywhere near a blade."

She snorted. "Then I'm sure I would've been a witch."

"An angel like yourself would've preferred to be the villain in the story?" For the first time, Father Gerard didn't look Loren directly in the eye. He balled and unballed his fist. His square jaw looked sharp at the edges.

Loren didn't seem to notice the change in his attitude. "Merlin and Morgan le Fay were always my favorites in the story. I've never understood why magical people are always villainized in stories, especially the women."

"Because men are afraid of women with power," I said.

Father Gerard shook his head. His jaw and fist relaxed. "I think both men and women are afraid when godly powers fall into their hands. Look at Pontius Pilate. Did you know he lobbied to spare our Holy Prophet? It was the crowd, the mob mentality, and their fear of the salvation Jesus brought to them that forced Pilate's hand and sent Jesus to the cross."

It took everything in me not to call bull on that. Pontius Pilate was not a man—not a human one at least. He was an Immortal who liked to meddle in the affairs of human religion and spirituality.

Yod, the eighth oldest Immortal, had been a

feature of the Sanhedrin since its inception. The Sanhedrin was the court system of ancient Israel. The judges were said to have been given full authority over the Israelites by God, and so the people were to obey every instruction and law established by the judges.

When Yod, then going by the name of Pilate, saw my friend Yeshua's influence growing over the people, he decided to exert his own influence to stop it. He didn't accuse the man himself. No, he was often recorded as being an advocate who tried to get Yeshua freed. But I'd seen Yod work his forked tongue before. I knew he'd been behind the execution of one of the world's greatest philosophers and prophets. A man who could've done so much more to save the hearts, minds, and souls of mankind if he had lived amongst the people longer.

Yeshua wasn't the first, nor was he the last. I believed Yod had a hand in many of the great prophets' untimely deaths, including Moses, Mohamed, and Siddhartha to name a few. He was the one Immortal I gladly kept my distance from for reasons other than the allergy that wracked our bodies when we stayed too long in one another's presence.

"We are human, not gods," continued Father

Gerard. "Such power is far above our comprehension, and if we encounter anything resembling it, it terrifies us. That is why mankind has always turned to God."

"There was a time when humans didn't think they could conquer fire, the sea, or the air," I said. "You thought those things more powerful than yourselves."

"Why do you say *you* as though you aren't human?" Father Gerard asked curiously, his gaze sharp.

I shrugged at my slip of the tongue. "Just making an argument. My point is that the sea has more power than you, yet you entrusted yourself to it."

"And when it overwhelmed me, I prayed. And an angel came my way." He turned to Loren.

Swayed by the celestial compliments, and a victim of a short attention span that failed to remind her that this man was more interested in her soul than getting in her pants, Loren leaned in toward him again.

"You said you were on a quest for knights?" I asked.

"Yes," he said. "There was a news story a couple of weeks ago where a farmer in Shropshire found something strange down a rabbit's hole. It turned out to be an underground temple. I think it may have belonged to the Knights Templar."

"The Templars?" Loren asked. "They were the medieval knights who protected Christian pilgrims on their journey to the Holy Lands, right?"

Father Gerard nodded. "In return, Pope Urban II promised that those brave and devout men would be forgiven for all their sins if they went on a crusade to win back Jerusalem for the heavenly father."

Yeah, no. It wasn't that simple. But like I'd been doing all day with history I had firsthand knowledge of, I held my tongue. It was clear the former priest admired the Templars. People didn't like it when someone told a very different truth about their heroes, truths that cast those they thought brave and devout into a sinister light.

"So, you're headed down a rabbit hole?" Loren asked. "What do you hope to find?"

Father Gerard's eyes went wide like a kid seeing the bounty underneath the Christmas tree. "The Templars were entrusted with many biblical artifacts. They were rumored to have brought them back to England for safekeeping as the wars and conflicts continued in the Holy Lands. If it's true, then who knows what could be there? An ancient copy of the Bible. The Spear of Destiny. The Holy Grail."

I knew for a fact that the original copy of the Bible was not in some underground rabbit hole, but there had been a spear used when Yeshua had been hung up on the cross. It was a longstanding practice during crucifixion to pierce the side or the legs to hasten death. It was possible the actual spear had been saved and secreted away somewhere. If so, I'd love to get my hands on it.

It wasn't that I believed it was magical. Most of the artifacts I sought weren't. To me, history and the stories contained in its remnant objects were the real magic.

But the Holy Grail? The cup Yeshua used at the Last Supper, which might also be the same cup that caught his blood as he bled from the cross, had been in the keep of The Arthur and his Knights for hundreds of years in the fortress known as Tintagel, more commonly called Camelot. It wasn't in a rabbit's hole that may or may not have been a hidey-hole for misguided knights.

"If you like adventure," Father Gerard said, an air of enticement lacing his deep voice, "you can tag along. I could use a sidekick."

"Umm..." Loren said, sounding thoughtful.

Umm? Was my bestie about to ditch me for a dude? Again?

"No," she said after a full minute.

Good. Because the Father was likely on a fool's errand. The Templars had disbanded in the early thirteenth century. Whatever was down that hole couldn't have been their doing, since another band of knights had kicked them out of England hundreds of years ago. And that band who sat at a round table had looted most of their wares, including the Grail.

CHAPTER FOUR

The storm stayed at bay as we made our way up the British Isles. The wind was light and the currents calm. I put the boat in reverse and took a sharp turn. Instead of skidding, the boat pivoted and we coasted neatly into a docking space.

We'd radioed ahead, and emergency personnel met us on the pier. They took the captain and his mate into a medical vehicle. The men thanked us profusely for our help on the waters, leaving me feeling a little more vindicated. When I turned to Father Gerard, his gaze was solely fixed on Loren.

"I suppose this is goodbye for now, Ms. Van Alst."

"For now?" Loren said. "Don't tell me you believe in fate, Father. Isn't that blasphemy against your God?"

"No. Fate is the handiwork of God. And the Creator sends us his angels disguised as ordinary people. Though I have the feeling you're anything but ordinary, Loren."

Loren tilted up the side of her mouth. Her chest rose as she inhaled to receive the praise. The holy man's eyes didn't miss it.

"So, yes," Father Gerard said, his voice hardening, "I have every faith that fate will bring us back together again. Until then, Ms. Van Alst, Dr. Rivers."

After one last lingering look, Father Gerard joined his crew in the emergency vehicle. The van pulled off, and I turned to Loren.

"You sure know how to make an impression on people," I said.

"What can I say? I'm extraordinary."

"You're also no angel."

"Hell, no, I'm not." She smirked.

We hired a car service and headed out on the road to make our way to Caerleon. After weeks of every color of blue on the seas, the greenery was blinding. Branches stretched to the sky with leaves blowing in the wind. Blades of grass carpeted the ground as far as the eye could see, rising up hillsides and rolling down the other side.

Caerleon had been the site of a Roman legion at the start of the last millennium. We drove by the remains of a grassy amphitheater and baths. For once, the sight of aged stones stretching up from the ground didn't entice me to whip out a shovel and dig. Instead, I made a beeline for the small village on the outskirts of the city.

Beyond the ruins, the rest of the city looked like a typical British suburb with houses spaced out a few acres apart. But that was only to the naked human eye. I was more than human.

We parked in an open spot in the town square. Shops and vendors lined the main street. A few tourists walked with travel brochures stuck in their faces and cameras slung over their shoulders. They were either on their way to see the Roman remnants behind us or the medieval castle in front of us. What they didn't see was the magic on display before them.

The town residents went about their daily business. A shopkeeper adjusted the items in her display window. The items levitated from one place to another and then back again as she changed her mind about the placement. But to the human eye, it looked as though she had pushed away and picked up the pieces with her hands.

The sliding doors of the grocery store were plastered with posters that read "Potions: Fifty Percent Off." But to the naked eye, the word "potions" looked like "lotions."

Children of various ages played in a schoolyard. Many of them moved at superhuman speeds in a game of tag. Others drew energy from the ground and made designs in the air that looked like small fireworks coming from the tips of their fingers. Walking through the streets of the magical town of Caerleon was like walking through a live action Harry Potter book, if one was so inclined to see the magical side of things.

"Oh my god." Loren stopped in her tracks. "It looks like that kid is levitating."

I looked over to a young witch who was indeed levitating. To the few tourists milling about the city, they'd only see a little girl on a hoverboard, the type that could be bought from an online retailer. But to someone whose mind could tap into the ley energy running under this city, they would see the young witch floating with her witch mother tugging on her hand to not go so high.

I stared at Loren. Her gaze was fixed on the little witch. Loren blinked her eyes rapidly as though something was stuck in the corner of them. Then she opened her eyes wide and laughed.

"Oh," she said. "She's on a hoverboard. I'm seeing things. Maybe it's all that sea air."

Or maybe it was because she'd had a run-in with the supernatural world for the last few months, including a recent encounter with Greek gods. The goddess Demeter had held Loren's soul for safekeeping for a night during a battle and then returned it in the morning. Perhaps Loren's enhanced sight was a temporary side effect of participating in the ritual of the Chosen.

"It kinda looks cool." She grinned. "I want to try it."

Before she could make her way over to the kid, someone shouting behind us caught our attention.

"Gwin? Gwin, wait!"

We turned to see a dark-haired beauty with eyes that were a startling navy blue. The young woman was just a few inches shorter than me, which was easy since I was as tall as an Amazon. She had the type of curves that would never make it onto the cover of a women's fashion magazine, but would be the centerfold of any men's magazine. She came up short when she came face-to-face with Loren.

"Oh." She frowned. "My apologies. From behind,

you look just like my sister. From the front, a bit as well." She peered at Loren, cocking her head one way and then another.

In turn, I did the same to the woman. "Morgan?" I said. "Is that you?"

Morgan turned to me and stared. She didn't cock her head but rather looked at me head-on. Recognition was very slow to come to her eyes.

I wasn't offended. It had been about fifty years since I'd seen her last. She'd been a rambunctious teenager at the time. Now she was a grown woman.

"Nova?" Morgan said. "Nova Flueve?"

"I go by Nia now."

"I remember you." She grinned, a faraway look in her eyes for a moment. "You tried to take Arthur's scabbard during a jousting festival."

I hadn't tried to take it. I'd just wanted to get a look at it. But he'd laid the blade side of his sword on my hand the moment my fingers touched it. After that, he and I may have tousled a bit. And that tousle may have spilled into the jousting arena for all to see.

"Oh, it was epic." Morgan's navy-blue eyes glittered with mirth and delight.

She'd been a rebellious youth. I remembered her sneaking into the armory at night. I had been up and wandering around the castle. Because I'd been restless, not because I had been snooping. That night, I'd taught her a few tricks in the weapons room and then promptly got read the riot act by Arthur and put out on my ass for corrupting the youth.

"Morgan?" Loren asked. "As in Morgan le Fay? King Arthur's sister?"

Morgan's face contorted into absolute horror. "I am not related to that fascist. And he's not a king. His head's too big for a crown, anyway."

Loren looked to me, her brow a crinkle of confusion.

"It's a lot to explain," I said.

"Morgan?" another voice called from behind. This voice was airy and light, but it still held the same timbre as Morgan's husky tone. "Morgan, I've been looking everywhere for you."

We turned to see a woman float toward us. She didn't actually float, of course, but the ground seemed as though it didn't want to disturb her tread.

Where Morgan was a dark beauty, this woman looked as though she'd stepped out of a ray of pure sunshine. She had the same dark-blue gaze, but honey-golden locks framed her heart-shaped face. She moved like a dancer with lithe, long steps. Her body was the type to grace the covers of fashion magazines from Paris to Rome to New York.

Her kind gaze settled on me. "Oh, Dr. Flueve? Is that you?

"Hello, Gwin." I reached out my hands to her. The last time I'd seen her had been on her wedding day.

"Gwin? As in Guinevere?" Beside me, Loren choked.

"It's been so long." Gwin smiled as she took my hands.

"This is my friend, Loren."

Loren wiggled her fingers but remained mute. It was the first time I'd ever seen her starstruck.

After offering Loren a friendly smile, Gwin looked around. Her eyes clouded with concern. "Does The Arthur know you're here?"

"Yes," I said. "I was invited."

"Really?" Morgan and Gwin said, both sounding surprised.

Admittedly, The Arthur and I didn't have the best relationship. His father and I had gotten along fairly well. The Arthur before that, the one most of the stories were attributed to, had been mostly cordial to me. I'd been a favorite of his great-grandfather, Uther. But the fourth king of Camelot, this current leader of the Knights and protector of witches and mystical objects? Yeah, he and I didn't always see eye to eye.

"Apparently, he needs my expertise. About the problem with the Grail?" I hedged, trying to get information from the sisters.

Both of their blue gazes turned vacant, void of any further details. It didn't surprise me when neither added to the conversation. Details about the Grail and any other artifact in possession of the Knights were a closely held secret.

"You know he doesn't tell us witches anything." Morgan crossed her arms over her chest. Distaste rang loud in her tone. "Just as much as he strong-arms you, he keeps us poor, defenseless women on a tight leash."

"He's just trying to protect us, Morgan," Gwin said softly. "These are trying times for us all."

"They are?" I asked, but she looked away from my inquisitive gaze.

Trying times? I couldn't fathom what that might mean. Witches and wizards had enjoyed a long peace for the last hundred years or so. Even before that, during the time of witch hunts and trials, actual witches hadn't suffered much, if at all. The knights were their ardent protectors against magical and human foes alike. They kept them safely hidden away behind magical shields and inside enchanted castles.

Gwin hadn't been alive during many of the witch trials of early Europe. She and Morgan were still young. Gwin, I knew, was about a century and a half. Whereas, I believed Morgan was pushing a century. And as far as I knew, neither woman had ever left the protection of Camelot and the knights who would lay down their lives for any of the people within its walls.

Which wasn't unusual. Witches and wizards preferred to keep to ley lines where their magic was strongest. But Caerleon wasn't the only line in the world. There were dozens of places that were pockets of energy.

"I'm sick of all this chivalry," Morgan fumed. "I wish it would crawl down a dark hole and die. Like up Arthur's a—"

"In your case, Lady Morgan," said a deep male voice, "chivalry went the same way as ladylike behavior."

We all turned around to see two men on horseback. Lance looked every bit the medieval knight upon his steed, even in blue jeans and boots. His ginger locks blew off his face in the light breeze.

His lips quirked up as he looked down at the four women before him.

Beside him another knight whom I knew to be Geraint swept his dark gaze across the few tourists milling about the streets. Whereas Lancelot's hair and beard were ginger thanks to his Scottish heritage, Geraint's black hair, charcoal beard, and brown skin pointed to his Moorish heritage.

None of the people on the street took any notice of two men riding with swords at their hips and shields strapped to their mares. Thanks to the shield charm I knew had been put in place by the strongest witches in the city, the tourists would only see two police officers on horseback.

Morgan turned a sickly-sweet smile up at Lance. "All I'm saying is that women's liberation has hit every corner of the world except our little town. You men keep us on short leashes."

"Whenever humans managed to get their hands on witches," Lance said, "trials and burnings tended to ensue."

"On human women," countered Morgan. "An actual witch would've taken them down."

"And then exposed us all to them, bringing them to our door." Lance's voice was even but firm.

"Humans far outnumber us. Even with our power, we could not defeat a horde of them."

Morgan didn't have a comeback for that one, because it was true. It was the reason most beings who were magical or supernatural kept to the shadows of the world. We were powerful, but humans were dangerous.

"And during these dark times," Lance continued, "we can't be too cautious."

Again with the trying and dark times. Camelot hadn't been under any form of attack since the end of the Middle Ages. Just exactly what was going on here? And what did it have to do with the Grail?

Lance's gaze turned from Morgan and connected with Gwin's, but only for a second before his eyes diverted to the ground. "My lady."

I had noticed Gwin sneaking covert glances at Lance while he'd engaged in verbal battle with her sister. But the moment the knight's attention turned to her, she'd averted her gaze as well.

"I trust your journey with our lord went well?" Lance asked.

Gwin opened her mouth. But before she could speak, her lip trembled. She turned her gaze to the horizon and gave a shake of her blonde head.

Lance looked as though he wanted to jump

down off his horse and take her into his arms. Instead, his fingers clenched around his lead and his jaw tightened. "I am sorry you had to witness the darker side of humanity, my lady."

"I'm glad I could be of service," she said. Her voice was small, but she managed to hold her chin up. Her gaze connected with Lance's for longer than was prudent before she looked away again.

Lance cleared his throat and adjusted his seat. Then he turned to me. "Dr. Rivers, I was sent to give you and your friend an escort from the town visitor's center, but it seems you made your way around."

I shrugged unapologetically. Like Morgan, I had no intention of being manhandled or led by a leash during my stay.

"I'll alert the boss that you're here." Lance gave a signal and his horse took off, followed by the watchful Geraint.

"Well, we need to return to our work," Gwin said. "We'll see you at last meal?"

I nodded. Gwin and Morgan took off, leaving me with an inquisitive Loren. As we walked toward the castle, I began to explain.

CHAPTER FIVE

The city had changed much since the last time I was here. Concrete was laid over the streets instead of gravel and grass. There was no smell of manure with the plumbing running underfoot instead of being dumped in the alleyways. There were still many stone and wood buildings, but now there was steel in the structures. Energy still rose from the stores deep in the ground, but now power lines and cables ran overhead to distribute signals from the outside world.

The biggest difference was the skyline. There were tall buildings off in the horizon. Airplanes flew overhead. One of the last times I was welcome inside the castle through the front gates, and not slipping in through a back door, had not been here in

Caerleon. It had been in Scotland at what would become known as Stirling Castle.

There had been no structure higher than Stirling Castle. And that was the way Arthur, the second of his name, had wanted it. His impenetrable fortress had sat atop a crag called Castle Hill. It was surrounded on three sides by steep cliffs. Arthur's court had left the castle before the union with England. The structure remained. And since that time, Stirling Castle had been used as a royal residence, most notably by Mary, Queen of Scots.

Before Stirling, the Arthurian court of Camelot had set up shop in Glastonbury—its actual birthplace.

"So, wait?" interrupted Loren. "They just picked up the castle and moved it?"

"Pretty much." I nodded.

We were walking down the main street of the city as I recapped the two-thousand-year history of the magical castle and its people. The surroundings weren't the only thing about the city of Camelot that had changed. The people had undergone an evolution as well.

On the streets of present day Camelot, the residents wore a mix of modern fashions and clothing from the past. A group of teenagers passed us by. The boys were in dark jeans and tunic shirts. The girls wore lace bodices and shorts. A couple of them held devices in their palms and had buds in their ears.

There were a few elderly men in doublets, a quilted coat of arms, with a surcoat emblazoned with their rank or social position in the court. Some women wore kirtles—colorful, fitted dresses worn over blouses.

To the tourists snapping photos, the fashions likely looked like part of the town's medieval charm. They never would've dreamed that many of these garments and people were from times of old. That right here in modern day Caerleon was a real Medieval Times.

"How do you move a castle and all its people?" Loren asked.

"Magic," I answered.

Beneath our feet, the city of Caerleon rested on a ley line. A ley line was a pocket of energy. Some believed the energy was natural. Others believed those lines formed along the paths of places of great spiritual, cultural, or religious significance. Like a subway transportation grid, the lines formed a route that spanned great distances. Beings sensitive to these energy lines often converged on the lines and drew their power from the unseen source.

With the largest population of witches and wizards in the world, the people of Camelot could move their court anywhere on earth where a ley line existed. They'd moved the original castle, known as Tintagel, from Cornwall about fifteen hundred years ago to Glastonbury in Somerset, then to Stirling in Scotland, and it now rested in Caerleon in Wales, where the present Arthur, the third of his name, ruled.

Like his father Uther, Arthur the First had been a warlord, not a king. He'd been born in a marsh in Argyll and not in the romantic fable of Camelot. There had been a Merlin, but he was a she and her name was Mary, but everyone called her Mara, the Scottish name for Mary. Oh, and Mara was a witch.

"Merlin was a woman?" Loren sounded awestruck. "You are seriously blowing my mind."

"With Lady Mara's help, Arthur the First fought and won many great battles."

"So there were twelve battles, like in the stories?" Loren asked. "That part's real?"

I shrugged. "I don't know how many battles he fought. But I know a number of those on record, like the battles of the River Dubglas, were fought by Arthur the First and his father Uther."

The Pendragons, like many throughout English history, had a long and torrid relationship with Rome. Most of the fighting knights engaged in was to keep the Romans off their territories. I remembered that Mara had a great distaste for Romans, but I never came to know the reason why. Over the years and centuries, the court fortified itself. More and more magical beings came within its walls and under the protection of Arthur and his knights.

Witches and wizards, and even many without any magic, were perpetually persecuted by mankind, whether they were superstitious villagers, power-mad royalty, or the Church. When anyone wouldn't subscribe to a particular custom, law, or religion, they were deemed undesirable and their life became forfeit.

Arthur and Mara had protected these people for hundreds of years. Wizards and witches had increased life spans. Not as long as an Immortal's or as endless as a god's, but witches and wizards could live for hundreds of years if they stayed connected to the ley line. If they lived on the grid, they're lives would be long. Maybe a couple hundred years instead of five. If they stayed too long off the grid after centuries of the ley energy fueling them, that time would catch up with them sooner rather than later.

"Anyway," I said, "that's the true story of the Arthurian Legends over the last two thousand years in ten minutes."

"You forget so much stuff," Loren said. "How is it you remember all of that?"

"Because I wrote it down." And because I had a particular interest in the magical city of Camelot. There were many artifacts locked away in Tintagel Castle that I was itching to get my hands on. Just for a look.

"So did a lot of people," Loren said. "Many of these stories were written down. And some of the authors got a few of the details right."

"A lot of the stories about the Arthurian Legends are based on a modicum of truth. History tends to repeat itself."

"The events and the names, apparently," said Loren. "Three Arthurs. There's a Lancelot and a Guinevere."

"But they're not the original people. For the men of court, those names are typically titles. *The* Lancelot. *The* Gawain. They're all from the lineage, but it got confusing to have so many people with the same name. So when the man—be it their father or uncle or cousin—passed on, the heir took the title and became *The* Galahad."

"What about the women?"

"I guess those names are just popular." I shrugged. "Like Mary and Joseph."

"No, I mean the daughters of the knights. Do they take on the names when they become knighted?"

"There's never been a female knight."

Loren's face contorted in disgust. "I'm seeing Morgan's point. That's sexist."

"Arthur's old-school. He sees women as damsels meant to be protected, especially if she's a witch. He would never let a woman anywhere near a sword and shield."

"Guinevere did seem like the type to be kidnapped by a villain and await rescue. I'm sure he loves that about his wife."

"Gwin's not married to Arthur," I said. "She married his brother…" I paused for dramatic effect. "Merlin."

"Ooh, the plot thickens." Loren rubbed her hands together. "And you saw that tension between Lance and Gwin?"

I did. I'd seen it between them when they were younger. I had no idea why neither of them had acted on it. Nor why she'd chosen to marry Merlin instead of Lance.

"Oh, I wish my mother could've seen this." Loren looked wistful. "She loved these stories. To know that they're real…"

Loren looked up to the heavens, as though in silent communion with her dearly departed. I gave her the quiet moment of reflection and studied the sight in front of us. We'd arrived at our destination, Tintagel Castle.

A group of tourists stood in front of the dilapidated castle, taking pictures in front of the ruins. The face of the castle was crumbling. It looked like a Jenga puzzle that would blow over with a small cough. There were hazard signs barring people from crossing the well-worn drawbridge to get across the swampy moat to the other side. A few teens stood apart from the group.

"This is so lame," said one of the teens.

"Oh, come on, sweetie," cajoled a mom in a fanny pack. "Look, there's a sword in a stone. Go on. Try to pull it out. It'll be fun."

The kid rolled his eyes. "Can't we go to Stonehenge instead? I heard they sacrificed people there. That sounds cool. This is just a pile of rocks."

"What's that kid talking about?" Loren asked, looking up at the ruins with wide eyes. "That's the most beautiful castle I've ever seen in my life."

I glanced around at the other few tourists standing near. None of their attention was on the wonder of architecture before them, nor should it have been. No one could see what I saw. Unless they were touched by the supernatural.

I turned back to Loren. The breeze carried the smell of fresh water from the nearby river that ran into the pristine moat encircling the castle. The sun warmed the skin on my forehead. The rays settled into the creases as I stared at my best friend.

"Loren, what do you see?"

"I see real turrets." Her face was lit brighter than the sun. "I've never seen a castle in such good shape. It's like it was built this century, not hundreds of years ago. The stones are immaculate and gleaming. They look like marble, not stone."

The residual effects of Demeter holding her soul must still be working. There was an enchantment on the castle, another of the witches' shields to keep humans out. Only those with magic could see the real face of the pristine palatial estate.

"Come with me," I said.

We headed away from the tourists. Bypassing the hazard signs, we crossed over the drawbridge that looked as though most of it had fallen into the moat below. In reality, the bridge was fully intact. Loren didn't hesitate a single step. In fact, she nearly skipped across to the doors of the castle.

A moat was not a decorative facet of castle living. The water was a deterrent for getting to the structure. As an added layer of protection, if the enemy tried to dig their way into the castle grounds, any tunnel would fill with water from the moat and collapse. But Loren and I walked straight across. No one stopped our advance into the main gate.

In ancient times, the iron gate with its ragged portcullis was literally a death trap. Attackers would enter and have the gates dropped down on their heads. If they escaped the jaws of the gates, they would next be met with arrows in the courtyard. A medieval castle was far more than a palace. It was a fortress ready-made for battle.

When I'd come here in the past, the drawbridge had not dropped down for me. I'd been met with swords at this gate. Then a contingency of knights as I was disarmed and escorted inside.

The doors were thrown wide open and

unguarded today. Only those who could *see* would even notice the entryway. I brushed my hand over the blade that never left my hip. I doubted any knight would actually raise his sword to gut me. But they would, and had, threatened me in the past. Over misunderstandings, of course.

To me, Camelot was a living museum. And like in most museums, people were supposed to look and not touch. I may have gotten a little too close to a tenth-century painting once. When I took it off the wall, the knights had misunderstood that it had been for inspection, not to take it. Even though I'd already crossed the threshold of the castle with it in my arms when we'd had our little skirmish.

Inside the doorway, both Loren and I gaped like tourists. Instead of my blade, I itched for a camera to document everything I saw before me. It wasn't as though they left their magical treasures out for anyone to view. No, I marveled over the everyday items that these people took for granted.

Just the flooring alone had me salivating. I only barely stopped myself from bending down and taking a sample. I ogled the candlesticks and torches hanging from the sconces. The metalwork was breathtaking. Even the tapestries were original. I reached out to touch the intricate stitching on the fabric. Before my fingers made contact, a dagger implanted itself in the fleshy part of my hand between my thumb and forefinger.

"Ouch," I wailed.

Loren withdrew her cane and pressed the button that released the blade of the sword within the device.

"Hands where I can see them," grumbled a voice deeper than a bear's.

I turned and looked at the hulking figure coming at me. If I were a lesser woman, or even a bear, I would've run. Instead, I clenched my bleeding fist and prepared to meet this foe.

"Good to see you, too, Arthur."

CHAPTER SIX

*A*rthur slow-marched down the winding stairs. His gait reminded me of a cowboy from the Wild West, though he wore no chaps. His powerful thighs were covered in dark breeches that hugged him from his calves on up to his gluteus maximus. His washboard abs and large pecs pushed against the fabric of his cotton tunic, which gaped open at his chest as though he'd hastily thrown it over his head. But my attention skated over these details—mostly. My gaze caught on the long, thick, broad blade swinging at his side.

So did Loren's. "Is that...?" Her own blade lowered as the finger of her other hand rose. She pointed at the fabled sword.

As though it wanted to answer for itself, the

sword caught a wayward ray of sunlight and flashed at us. It might, in fact, have a mind of its own. Excalibur was a magical object, after all.

The story about the sword being plunged into stone was fabricated. What was true, though, was the fact that the magical blade chose the person who would wield it. It was the same with every knight's weapon. The magic would only respond to an owner of its choosing. And that magic was the ability to wound other things that were magical or supernatural. Like me.

Arthur reached the last rung of the steps. He didn't move fast. He didn't need to, just as a mountain had no need for speed. His sheer size was imposing enough.

Arthur, the third of his name, was a massive male. A hulking specimen of manhood. Imagine if Thor and Hulk had a baby. Yeah, this dude, blocking out the sun as he made his way toward me, was still bigger.

He was made much like his warrior ancestors. The Pendragon genes were still stuck in the fifth century. The males hadn't evolved into the lanky, lean metrosexuals of modern day. Arthur was built to withstand the harshness of a world filled with magic, monsters, and powerful entities that any human would piss their pants in the face of. And now he stood before me, looking none too pleased.

I didn't bother with my dagger. I wasn't this man's favorite person in the world because of, well, misunderstandings in the past. But I also knew he would never raise that sword against me.

Remove me bodily? Sure.

Lash me with his tongue—and not in the good way? Been there, done that.

But his code of chivalry prevented him from killing me.

Probably.

I was pretty sure.

He might toss a dagger or a throwing star at me. But only to maim. He knew I was tough to kill.

I pulled the blade from my hand. Though I was Immortal, I could be wounded. Most of the time, those wounds were superficial and never permanent. They'd heal up within a few hours. Or if they were severe by human standards, in a few days. As long as I wasn't around someone of my own kind. With the allergy that existed between Immortals, our bodies made us kryptonite to one another. If we were exposed to one another for too long, we could die.

Arthur wasn't immortal. Neither was he a wizard.

He was a man with witches in his ancestral line. That made him stronger than a human, as strong as an Immortal, but slightly more breakable.

I held Arthur's blade between us. My blood glinted in the sunlight. "That hurt."

"You'll live," he said.

"Aren't you supposed to be chivalrous to women?"

"I aimed for your hand and not your heart, didn't I?"

I tossed the weapon back at him.

He caught it between two fingers, holding it next to his square chin. His jaw was covered in a dark golden beard that matched the shoulder-length locks that brushed the tops of his shoulders.

"You called, I came," I said. "And this is how you treat your guests?"

He breathed a harsh laugh. His gray eyes turned to hard steel.

"Are you still mad about the scabbard debacle?"

His jaw worked. He tilted his head to the side, and I heard a crack. "During your time here, you will confine yourself to the first floor and the guest quarters. Any locked doors are locked for a reason. That would include my bedroom door as well."

Beside me, Loren gasped. When I turned to her,

she had an approving smile on her face. Thank god she didn't hold up her hand for a high five.

I shook my head in denial. "It was a misunderstanding. I was looking for an ancient Saxon sword hilt."

"Sure you were," Arthur drawled.

"I had a boyfriend at the time," I said. "I don't. Anymore. Have a boyfriend, I mean."

It was so weird saying it. But it was the first time I'd said it out loud. Beside me, Loren nodded sympathetically. She gave me an encouraging smile as though I'd just admitted the first step out of twelve in an addicts' program.

Arthur, on the other hand, looked as though he wanted to be anywhere but here having this touchy-feely conversation with two women.

"You're here at my pleasure," Arthur said gruffly. "When I become displeased, which I'm sure will happen all too quickly, you will be removed."

"You really know how to sweet-talk a girl, Artie."

But he was done with me. He turned his attention to Loren. "Who's this?"

"She's with me," I said.

"A new Immortal?" Arthur asked.

"Oh, no. I'm all human," Loren gushed. As her pitch went higher, so did her chest. But it was how

Loren greeted any man she took an ardent interest in. "I'm one-hundred-percent woman. My name's Loren Van Alst. And I'm a huge fan, Your Liege."

Loren took a deep bow, which just so happened to show off her cleavage, giving both Arthur and me a clear view down the suddenly unbuttoned top of her shirt.

Arthur looked. Of course he looked. He was a male. But he was a courtly knight above all else.

"I've already had a trying day." He turned on his heel before she straightened. "Let's get this over with."

Arthur held out his hand for us to precede him. I grabbed Loren's forearm and yanked her up to standing. We walked in front of Arthur.

"Is he gay?" Loren whispered loud enough for our object of gossip to hear.

"No," I said. "He just has a warped sense of honor."

At the end of the hall, Arthur stepped before us to open the great door. I knew what lay behind the massive wood door. It was what used to be the throne room of this castle hundreds of years ago when the title of king still applied to the mortal world. But the throne was short-lived. The chair had truly been replaced with a—

"Oh. Em. Gee. Nia, look. It's the Round Table." Loren bounced on her toes and pointed like the tourists we'd seen outside.

Inside the room, a group of men turned to observe us. Just like out on the main street of town, looking around the room was like staring through a kaleidoscope that mashed up medieval times and the modern world.

The assembled men wore a mix of breeches, jeans, and dress pants. They were an assortment of skin tones, facial features, body sizes, and ages. But every single one of them looked as though they patronized the same barber. Beards and long hair were the fashion for the ages.

Lance leaned against the back of one chair next to Geraint. Across from them stood the golden-haired Tristan. He'd been just a boy the last time I was here, but he'd grown into a handsome young man since then. His father sat in the chair next to him. The man was well past his prime, but like a few other knights of old, his counsel was still of immense value to the knights who'd taken on their titled names.

I recognized Sir Kay and Sir Bedivere, both the third of their names. Neither had produced male heirs. Because of their age, they couldn't stay too long off the ley line or they would expire quickly.

"There are a lot of empty seats," Loren said, looking around at the sparsely attended meeting.

"It's likely that some of the knights are out on quests," I said. "But some lines are no longer represented because they died out."

I turned to Arthur, who had made his way to the seat of his father. It was marked with the name that they both shared.

"Your brother, Merlin, I trust is on a quest?" I said. "What are you guys looking for this time? The Spear of Destiny?"

Silence. The room had quieted when we'd come in. But this silence spread dark, ominous tendrils out across the room.

"My brother was lost to us on a quest twenty-five years ago."

"I'm so sorry. I didn't know."

Poor Gwin. I didn't even ask after him when I'd seen her earlier. But then again, I hadn't known he'd passed away.

"That is part of the reason you're here," Arthur said. "For the last few years, witches and wizards who live off the ley line have disappeared. Some have been murdered."

"Murdered? Like in the witch hunts of old?"

"Not exactly," Lance said. "We know who this enemy is. They're organized, they're old, and they know how to overtake and destroy something with magic."

"Who?" I asked.

"A witch was murdered just this morning," he said. "Lady Circe lived in Cenote Sagrado."

The Sacred Cenote was a well in Mexico also known as the Well of Sacrifice. It was a holy place to the ancestors of the Maya where the people worshiped a rain god. It was also believed to be a major pocket of ley energy. Now that Arthur confirmed that a witch had lived there, I took that belief to be a truth.

"We received a distress signal from her," Arthur continued.

"How?" Loren asked eagerly. "She came to you in a vision?"

"No," Arthur said, looking as if he wanted to roll his eyes, but he refrained. "She called us on her cell phone. All she was able to say was, *they're here.* By the time we arrived, her body had been burned."

His words chilled me to my very bones. I'd been alive during the worst of the witch hunts. It was an awful time in human history. So that was what

Gwin and Lance had meant earlier about dark times. But who was committing these crimes against witches?

"Take your seats," Arthur said. "Time is of the essence."

I went for one of the guest seats at the table. Loren went for the empty seat of Galahad.

"No." I stayed her hand. Only a named knight could sit in a claimed chair. "Don't sit there. Sit in one of the unmarked chairs." I indicated one to the side, near the wall. She pouted, but for once, she did as she was told.

"There was a tunnel found in Shropshire," Arthur began.

I jerked back. "Wait? Is this about the bunny hole that led to what people believe is a Knights Templar temple?"

The knights were silent. My gaze bounced from bearded face to bearded face. A few of the men's jaws clenched at the name of the group.

"Come on," I said. "That can't be real. We all know the Templars disbanded in the 1300s."

Again, silence.

"All right," I said. "I'm listening."

"We've been searching for that temple for hundreds of years," Arthur said. "We believe it contains information that will lead us to the resting place of the Grail."

"But the Grail is here. Your father said so."

"He lied," Arthur said.

I tilted my chin down and frowned. "That wasn't very chivalrous of him."

"What would you have done if my father had told you it was taken from here for safekeeping hundreds of years ago?"

Now I didn't respond. We all knew what I would've done. I'd have searched the world for it if it was no longer on the hallowed, impenetrable grounds of Camelot. Just to have it as part of my collection. It was only a cup. But the significance people gave it made it priceless. And I was a bit of a hoarder for items with historical significance.

"So where is it?" I asked.

Arthur took a deep breath. "We don't know exactly."

"Seriously? I've been snooping around this place for hundreds of years and what I was looking for wasn't even here? And now you tell me you don't know where it is either? Well, that's just bad manners."

"As long as the secret was kept, there was no danger," Arthur said. "But now with the temple found, if anyone gets to the Grail before we can recover it..."

"But it's just a cup," I insisted. "It doesn't have magical powers."

"The Grail is a revered object. Its resting place has been on a ley line for hundreds of years. The reverence of the devout as well as the potency of the ley line give it an awesome power."

I leaned in, elbows on the table. "To do what exactly?"

"It doesn't matter," Arthur said tersely. "All that matters is that it doesn't fall into the wrong hands."

"And those hands would be the Templars? But, I say again, they disbanded hundreds of years ago."

Arthur shook his head. "They are alive and thriving."

"They are the ones responsible for the disappearances and murders," Lance added.

I turned back to Arthur. "But didn't the Templars and your grandfather work together? Weren't they the original keepers of the Grail?"

"It's true," Arthur said. "Once, the Knights of Camelot and the Knights Templar fought on the same side against those who would have used the power gifted to my people for evil. But when the Templars' leadership changed, the organization grew corrupt. They've been waging a war against magic since the twelfth century. When my ancestors saw that they were turning away from the light, they took the Grail from here and sequestered it in a safer place. Unfortunately, that knowledge was lost to us."

"And now you want to go down the rabbit's hole to recover it?"

Arthur nodded.

"What's the matter? You guys too big to fit? Why do you need me?"

"We suspect that the language the directions are written in is ancient."

"Oh…" I leaned back in the chair. "So what you need is a translator."

"Yes," Arthur said, opening his palms as though making an offer. "We have to move quickly. The media has sensationalized the find. There are crews and spectators all over the site. It's only a matter of time before the Templars find it."

"I'm sorry. We usually have guests stay in better accommodations." Gwin led Loren and me down a narrow hall in what must have once been the dungeon of the castle.

We'd gone down floor after floor, the staircase narrowing and narrowing. I knew that the stairwell of a castle was yet another battle tactic in its arsenal. Any attacker racing up a stairwell would naturally have their right shoulder, which so often happened to be their sword arm, against the interior of the wall, making it difficult to swing on any defenders coming down. The defenders coming down had the advantage of their sword arms being in the range of the outside wall, giving them room to swing.

Also, these steps were uneven. Some were longer,

others shorter. Some slightly higher and others a few inches shallower, causing a trip hazard. So if an attacker didn't know the pattern, they couldn't move quickly and would get overtaken if charged from above.

But Loren, Gwin, and I made our way to the guest rooms without tumbling head over feet. I'd stayed in this castle a few times over the past millennium. The lords and ladies of the castle often resided in the highest towers of the structure—solar chambers, they were called. They were the most luxurious and got the most heat.

Down in the dregs of the castle where the common folk resided was cold, dank, smelly, and loud. The windows, if one was lucky enough to have one, were tiny. The meager rays of sun would shine through glass... and then immediately drown in the cold stone of the interior. Fireplaces, again if lucky enough to have one, generated more smoke than heat. The toilet was a pot in the corner of the room —did I mention the smell already?

I dropped my bag in a room that wasn't exactly five-star, but neither was it fifteenth century. There was an AC unit on the wall. The thermostat read a cool sixty-eight degrees. There was no window, but the tapestries brightened the room. A lush comforter was spread over the king-sized bed. And a small three-piece bathroom was tucked in the corner. I wondered what the better accommodations Gwin spoke about were.

"Arthur insists that this is where you'll stay," Gwin said, her voice still apologetic. Gwin was the lady of the castle, having married the eldest of the Pendragon sons. Since Arthur had no wife, and didn't look as though he would take one anytime soon, it looked as though Gwin still maintained her hosting duties.

"It's better than I expected," I said. "I still don't have Arthur's full faith and trust."

"Well, you did try to steal the Seure from his right-hand knight," Gwin pointed out.

The Seure was an ancient sword used in a battle against the Saxons. I'd been on a dig with other archaeologists from SACS in a location believed to be where the great Battle of Edington occurred in the eighth century. Technically, it was Arthur's land, and technically, I was poaching. I'd gotten caught by Lancelot.

"I still say that sword belongs in a museum," I huffed.

"I'd have to agree with Arthur and the knights

there, Nia. Magic in human hands is dangerous. Even behind glass enclosures."

I raised my hand to counter, preparing to launch into my favorite argument about how history must be shared. That was the way we all learned from, and remembered, our mistakes and our successes. Another being who'd lived a long life had to know humanity tended to repeat itself even with the lessons laid out before them. But Gwin's kind smile morphed into concern. Her gaze fixed on my injured hand.

"What happened?" she asked.

"Oh, it's nothing," I said, waving away the injury. "Just a welcoming handshake from Arthur. It'll be healed before tomorrow morning."

"I can heal it now," Gwin said.

"It's not a big deal."

"I've never understood people who walk around in pain, especially when something can be done about it."

"I don't want to trouble you," I said, cradling my hand. "I know that healing can zap your energy."

Her hand had been outstretched to receive mine, but I saw a tremor there. Her gaze deflected from mine, and a dark shadow crossed her blue eyes. But it was just for a fleeting moment.

She inhaled and reached for my hand again. "It's just a minor wound. Really, it's no trouble at all."

I gave her my hand. She guided me over to the bed, and we sat side by side. Loren perched herself on the dresser and crossed her feet at her ankles, swinging her feet like a child.

"I was sorry to hear about your husband," I said.

Gwin nodded as she bent over my forearm. The magic she pulled from the ley line and sent into my injured hand was warm, like a fire in the middle of a snowstorm. "We were blessed to have as much time together as we did. When he was born, he had so much magic in him that his parents didn't expect him to make it through his first year, let alone one hundred."

Males born with magic were often frail creatures. With just a touch of power, they became a warrior. Big, brawny, and brave. The protectors of all things magical. But if too much magic coursed through a male child's veins, it could wrack his body, leaving him physically weak or even killing him.

Merlin had been one such child. Where his brother was easily the greatest warrior since his warlord great-grandfather, Merlin had been a sickly child, confined to the indoors and the bed for most of his young life as the magic took its toll on his form. But that had changed once Gwin was born.

Even as a child, she'd been the most gifted healer in the town. Her magic was likely what had kept Merlin alive for so long. I remembered the two being close, but I had never noticed any passion between them during my visits.

"He'd grown strong since the last time you'd seen him," Gwin said as she twisted my healed hand to and fro, inspecting her work. "He had always wanted to go on a quest, to help protect his people. But I disagreed. I insisted he wasn't strong enough, not as strong as..."

She took a deep breath and let it out slowly. I looked up to Loren. We could both guess who Merlin might've compared himself to in Gwin's eyes. But neither of us voiced our opinion.

"He said it wasn't a quest. It was a mission," Gwin continued. "That he was called by God."

Yes, the witches, wizards, and knights of Camelot believed in God. They followed the teachings of Jesus. The children were baptized. They went to church. They held the words from the Sermon on the Mount particularly close to their hearts. The one with all the blessings—*Blessed are the poor in spirit for theirs is the kingdom of heaven.*

"It was hard to argue with that, but I did. We quarreled before he left." Gwin took in a shaky breath as she continued to hold onto my healed hand. "His last memory of me was of his wife doubting him."

"Oh, Gwin." I squeezed her healing hand in return.

She clasped her hand over mine and pulled me in. Her voice was quiet, just above a whisper, as she spoke. Her eyes were wide with unshed tears when she said, "I don't think he's dead."

It took me a moment to run her words through my head. "But Arthur said he was taken by Templars, that they destroy anything and anyone magical."

"I can still feel him."

Gwin took her hands back and waved them in front of her heart. My own heart ached for her. I knew what it was like to be so entwined with another person that their presence could be sensed even from far away.

But something about the way she wrung her hands made me think it was more than just a wife's intuition. She didn't look reverent. She looked a touch afraid.

"What do you mean, you can feel him?" I asked gently.

She averted her gaze. "We have a connection." She blinked a couple of times, and I saw something in her close up. She swallowed before meeting my eyes. A smile was plastered on her face when she did. "I'm his wife, after all."

I would've bought that explanation, but her forced smile told me there was something she wasn't saying. Still, there was a flaw in her hope. "If he had survived, he wouldn't have been able to live off a ley line this long. What's it been? Twenty-five years?"

Merlin was over two hundred years old. Those years spent off a ley line would've caught up to him by now, and he would be dead. There was no way around that fact.

Gwin looked away and faced the tapestries on the walls. Before she did, I saw a slight glint in her eye as though a possibility existed, but she didn't share the answer.

"You're probably right," she conceded. "I'm just feeling overtaxed by the day's events. I'd never come face-to-face with those who would do harm to people who practice things they do not understand or do not agree with."

Gwin's eyes clouded over as a storm of memories

swept through her mind. I remembered her words with Lance from earlier. He'd asked about her journey, and she'd gotten the same look.

"Gwin? Did you accompany Arthur earlier when he...?" I didn't know how to complete the sentence, but I didn't have to.

Gwin nodded, averting her gaze. "I did. I had to open the ley line for the knights to travel. Merlin used to do it for them. I'm called on to do much for the city these days, in addition to healing, since my magic is the strongest."

She stopped and took another deep breath. I wanted to halt the conversation. She looked so taxed as she spoke.

"I'd known Circe when I was a little girl. She fell in love with a human and moved to Mexico." Gwin's lip trembled. Her hands went to her skirts. There was a smudge at the hem, as if the edges had been burnt.

I swallowed a gasp. All the tales of burning a witch to ensure their death had roots in real rituals. Witches and wizards burned their dead instead of burying them. When a magical being's spirit passed on, the body might die, but the magic never did. It would stay in the magical being's body, keeping them preserved for decades. But when the body was burned, the energy was transferred back into the ground to rejoin the ley energy from which it originated.

"We hear tales of war and death and the persecution of our kind in all the stories and history books, but to see it firsthand…" Gwin took a shaky breath and let it out slowly as though she could push the image of her dead friend from her mind. "Arthur is pulling all the witches and wizards back into Camelot until things become safe again. Which I hope will be soon."

She took another deep breath. This time when she blew it out, her face transformed. Her hostess smile was back in place.

"I need to go and help with the meal," she said. All talk of possibly alive husbands and deceased witches was gone. "You two get settled. I'll see you in the Great Hall in a few hours."

She rose and headed to the door. It shut behind her, and Loren and I looked at each other.

"Well," Loren said. "That was…"

"Yeah."

"She's over a hundred years old? I need to get the brand of her moisturizer."

Trust Loren to defuse a tense situation. "Time moves differently on the ley lines."

I rose from the bed, and she shoved off the dresser. We headed out the door. Loren fell in beside me as we made our way back up the narrow stairwell.

"Physically, Arthur looks like he's in his late twenties," I said. "But in actual years, he's closer to two hundred and twenty-five."

"So Merlin was the older brother?"

I nodded. "Arthur was the second-born son. It's the sword that chooses who carries the name, not the birth order. Excalibur chose him over Merlin."

We reached the upper floors and spilled out into another great hall. On the walls of these halls were portraits and paintings of the lords, ladies, and knights of the past.

There were paintings of Uther and Igraine. Paintings of Arthur, the first of his name, a dark-haired beauty who had been his wife Mara, and their children. I had only met the couple once, and Mara only briefly. But the rendition of the queen looked familiar. As someone who'd lived a long time and met countless people, that wasn't hard to say. But something in her eyes called to me.

Mara looked nothing like the Celtic beauties surrounding her. She had a rich skin tone, as though she'd spent time in a warmer desert clime. There was a tilt to her eyes, as though her ancestral line had passed through Asia. But I didn't have time to try to figure out what her heritage might be. There was something flying straight for my face.

A ball came streaking overhead and nearly collided with the painting. Loren reached out and grabbed it before it could make impact. The ball slowed and corrected course. Instead of hitting the wall, it landed in her hands.

"Neat trick," she said, looking up at the children on the stairs. "But hasn't anyone told you about playing ball inside?"

The kids all looked down, likely awaiting a tongue-lashing from an adult. Luckily for them, Loren barely passed for a grown-up.

"You gotta toss a ball from up high," Loren said, winking. "That way, it goes faster. It's physics."

She bounded up the steps amid the kids. I stared after her. I hadn't even known Loren liked kids, let alone got along with them. There was so much I didn't know about the woman.

"Nova? Is that you, my dear?"

I turned and saw a face from one of the paintings smiling at me from across the way. My feet were moving to her and I was in her arms before I could stop myself.

CHAPTER EIGHT

"It's good to see you too, sweet girl."

I allowed myself to be enfolded into an ample bosom and wrapped in short arms. But it felt as though my whole body was being embraced. The woman was shorter than me, and my head came to rest at the gray bun atop her head.

The painting on the wall of Arthur and Mara surrounded by their children and grandchildren had included a young girl with the raven hair of her grandmother Mara and the light eyes of her great-grandmother Igraine, the first of her name.

I released Igraine, the second of her name, and looked into a wizened face. Those were rare on a ley line where everyone looked young. But this woman was actually old. The first time I'd met her was a thousand years ago. She'd seen wars and peace and births and deaths. Unlike me, she remembered them all.

I allowed myself one more moment of her embrace. Igraine felt like home. Not my secret home out in the middle of the sea where I went to be alone. She felt like all the things I'd never had. All the comforts I'd read about when people had a family. All the families I'd seen but never had for myself.

Except when I was in this woman's arms. I never forgot her. She was one of the reasons I always eventually made my way back to this place.

She was also one of the reasons I dreaded coming here. I knew that one day I'd come to this magical land and there would be no warm hugs for me. Witches had long lives, but they weren't immortal.

"How are you, darling girl?"

She called me *girl* when in relative time, I was far older than she was. I opened my mouth to respond, to tell her about the digs I'd been on, the adventures I'd braved, and all the new artifacts I'd found. But what spilled to the forefront of my mind was the

death and destruction I'd left in my wake—
memories of my dead friend Vau, of the Lin Kuie, of
Greek gods and Spartan warriors, and the look on
Zane's face when he told me he didn't want to see
me anymore. All that came out of me was a choked
sob, and my eyes burned.

"Oh, dear." Igraine brought me back into her
bosom. "Let's get you a cup of tea."

I looked to the steps where Loren and the
children had disappeared and hesitated. But with
one tug of Igraine's gnarled hands, I followed.

She led me into the kitchens. There were so
many good smells that it knocked my knees out from
under me. My butt sank into a chair. And before I
knew it, a steaming mug was pressed into my hands.

Igraine was Arthur's aunt. Gwin might be the
lady of the castle, having married Merlin, but
Igraine was its heart and soul.

I told her the highlights of the last fifty years
since I'd seen her, sticking mostly to the last year,
which had been the doozy. She stirred large
cauldrons filled with rich vegetables and fresh meat.
Well, she didn't physically stir them. She waved her
hands, and the ladles turned circles in the large pots.
Children ran in and out, tugging at her apron strings

for this and that as she listened to me. And all the while, I never once felt like I didn't have her full attention.

I'd sat at this table many times over the years. The table wasn't always in this location, but it was the same. It had weathered hundreds of years, just like me. There were nicks and scars, but it was tough. Igraine came and sat down across from me.

In another time, Igraine's family would have sat around this table and laughed and joked. I'd been included a few times, but it always left me with such a heaviness in my heart when I left. There were so few people like me, and we could never manage such a thing. I'm not sure that we would want to even if we could.

"You had a family once," Igraine said, smiling at me as she stirred the stew on the stovetop. She said she couldn't read minds, but she could read faces like a gypsy read tea leaves. And sometimes, she saw things. "You had a mother and a father who loved you very much. You had to in order to get here."

I shrugged. I knew that traveling via birth canal wasn't the only way to enter this world.

"Did you know the Greek gods and goddesses weren't born in a human way?" They were brought into the world fully formed after the sacrifice of whole tribes of humans.

"Their birth process may be different, but they were conceived. Even if it was with just a thought."

"How was I conceived?" I asked, not expecting an answer. I was simply enjoying her voice and her company.

"You were conceived with love."

Every time we talked, we eventually came around to this topic and this very conversation. It was my favorite story, that I had a birth, a family, a mother who'd held me in her arms, a father who had rubbed his palm roughly on the top of my head before heading out to do...I wasn't sure. Fight dinosaurs?

"They'll be ready to forgive you soon."

I blinked and focused on Igraine. That wasn't a part of our normal diatribe. It usually ended with another hug and a refill of my tea.

Igraine was standing again. Her squat body was at the stove, holding the teakettle. The hot steam rose around her fingers, but she didn't put it down. I stood and rushed to her side.

"You will be allowed to return soon," she said, turning her face to me.

Her gaze was cloudy, her pupils dilated like she

was in a Chosen ritual. Magic permeated the air. I felt the change in the room like a thick heat as Igraine slipped deeper into her trance.

"Twelve were exiled," she said. "Only seven will return."

I stared at her. My breathing went shallow. My hands shook as though I were the one clutching a steaming kettle.

There were twelve Immortals. Or at least there had been. Only ten of us remained. We had no memory of where we came from, of what we were, or how we got here.

"Return?" I asked. "To where."

"To the garden."

"Garden? What garden?"

The teakettle screamed, and Igraine snapped out of the trance. She clutched her hand to her chest. The red marks stained her palm, and the skin blistered.

"I'll get Gwin," I said.

But Igraine stayed me with her other hand. She took her uninjured palm and swiped it over her throbbing red skin. The magic healed her instantly. Then her eyes focused on me.

"Did I have a vision?" she asked. Her eyes were full of regret.

Oftentimes what Igraine saw in the trancelike state was death and destruction. When she came out of it, she didn't always remember what she'd seen or said. If what she'd just said was true, more of my kind would die.

"No," I lied.

But Igraine was a mother, a grandmother, and an auntie to many. She cocked her head and stared until I came clean.

"You were talking about my family," I said. This entire city revolved around Igraine. I saw that just sitting at the kitchen table as people moved around her like she was the sun. "You told me that my parents loved me. I just wish I could remember them."

It wasn't exactly a lie. It just wasn't the whole truth.

"I'd like to leave behind a legacy," I said. "But I'll never have a family like this."

"We are all connected," Igraine said, leading me back to the table. "From those who were here before us until now. Witches, wizards, gods, Immortals. We are the highest expression of humanity."

"You have such an impact on people's lives," I said. "I feel like no one would miss me if I suddenly disappeared."

"Nonsense. Much of humanity would be wiped out, forgotten, lost, or still hidden if it wasn't for you. With your endless quests to uncover the lost truths and forgotten tribes, you've helped shape this world we all share."

She had a point. But no one sang my praises. There were no stories or poems written about me. When I left here again, I'd be all alone.

"Nia..." Loren burst through the door. "You won't believe what they have upstairs."

That wasn't true. I'd have Loren. Even if only for a few more years. If I got lucky, maybe a few decades.

Igraine stood and faced Loren. "My dear, if you aren't the spitting image of..."

Igraine ran her now healed hand down the side of Loren's face. Her eyes glittered with memory, not a trance. And then she laughed to herself. It was full of sorrow.

"But that's impossible," Igraine said.

Loren looked from me to the elderly woman. Her gaze rested on Igraine, studying her in return. "I don't know. I've seen a lot of impossible lately. Who do I remind you of?"

Igraine chewed at her lip another moment before continuing. "Let me show you."

She took Loren's hand and walked back out into

the great hall. I followed. We moved past the Pendragon paintings. Past Lancelot and his ginger-framed family to a blonde-haired bunch.

"This is the line of Galahad," Igraine said. "Galahad, the second of his name, had two daughters and no sons."

There was a family portrait of a woman with blonde hair and a man with dark hair. Between them sat a young Gwin and Morgan. But a closer look told me I was mistaken. Though the two women favored the sisters, their features weren't an exact match.

"That is Gwenhwyfar, Gwin and Morgan's mother." Igraine pointed to the dark-haired little girl. Then she turned her attention and her index finger to the second little girl. "This was his second daughter."

I heard Loren's intake of breath when she came face-to-face with the painting. Standing behind her, I would've sworn it was her reflection.

"Galahad's second daughter ran away from home about fifty years ago to be with a human male, an archaeologist. A Flemish man."

Flemish was an old-world term for Dutch.

"What's your father's surname, child?"

Loren didn't take her eyes off the painting. "Van Alst."

Igraine nodded.

"What was her name?" Loren asked, pointing to the blonde girl in the painting.

"Her name was Magda."

CHAPTER NINE

*L*oren's face blossomed like a plant that had been in a cold, shaded corner for a year of winters and now was getting its first taste of sunlight.

Igraine looped her arm around Loren's trim waist. My strong bestie who'd stood firm in a crowd of ninjas intent on tearing her apart, who'd flicked her hair at an irate Greek goddess bent on enslaving the world—that woman wilted. It was as though her body couldn't hold up the beautiful bloom that had suddenly sprouted from her person.

Igraine rubbed Loren's lower back as she began a tale of a precocious Magda who dreamed of traveling the world and ran off with a dashing young man who dug holes in remote, forgotten places for a living. As Igraine talked and rubbed, Loren's body unfurled and grew tall again.

They walked down the hall toward the setting sun. But I stayed rooted.

Both Loren and I had received unexpected news about our families today. Hers was welcomed, and she soaked up Igraine's words. I turned away and slunk into the shadows of the castle walls.

Had Igraine's vision been real? *Twelve were exiled. Only seven will return.* Who had exiled us? Were there more people like us? And if so, where? I'd been in every inhabitable place on this earth, and I'd never met any Immortal other than the twelve.

Exiled? From a garden? But what tripped me up the most was the reentry fee. Only seven would return.

There were ten of us left since Vau and Epsilon had been murdered. It was nearly impossible to kill an Immortal. The only way to do it was to weaken us through proximity to one another. But that had only happened once, and it had been a fluke dozens of years in the making.

It couldn't be a literal vision. In any case, my head hurt just thinking about it. I hated riddles.

I wandered the lower floors of the castle. It was

uncanny how many things I forgot over my lifetime, but I could always find my way to a weapons room. My feet led me into the armory. The smell of steel and leather and the faint tinge of blood instantly lifted my spirits.

Medieval weaponry coated the walls. There was a case of modern and revolutionary guns under lock and key in the corner. Electronic gadgets and gizmos were splayed out in another case. Weights, punching bags, and sparring dummies were tucked neatly into another corner.

I ignored all the modern toys and headed to the wall of swords. They were all strung up by their hilts. The leather handles looked like soldiers in a straight line with their bulbous chests proudly protruding, ready to be taken into service.

There was an array of single blades and doubles, some curved, others straight. A line of arming swords caught my eye. These I knew were lightweight and well-balanced weapons that allowed excellent thrusting in combat.

Above them hung broad swords with straight, two-edged blades favored by cavalrymen. On one side of the broad swords were falchions, sickled blades that were reminiscent of a machete but topped with a cross guard. To the other side were heavy long swords. A soldier, or knight, would need both hands to swing such a beautiful weapon.

"Leave your hands where I can see them."

I looked over my shoulder at the sound of the deep voice. Arthur came out of the corner. He was shirtless. Cotton pants hung low on his lean hips. Sweat dripped down from his chest until it met the waistband of his pants. Either from his movement or from his sweat, the waistline looked slogged and slipped down further. His feet were bare. That was what struck me as the most intimate—his long toes striking the hard floor.

"Don't worry," I said. "I'm probably the only woman here not interested in playing with your toys."

He quirked an eyebrow. At the moment, his dirty-blond hair brought to mind a Viking god instead of a Celtic warrior.

My gaze glanced off his defined chest and went over his shoulder to the swords on the opposite wall. "Okay, that's not entirely true."

He grabbed the hilt of an arming sword. He rotated his wrist, and the blade of the sword whistled a tune as it cut through the air. "You think you can take me?"

Now I smirked. From the Iron Age to the Internet

Age, I'd had men flirt with me. They used every manner of pick-up line from *What a fine set of chalices you have* to *Is your name Wi-Fi? Because I'm feeling a connection*. But in any period, if a man challenged me to a duel, their long sword had a better chance of getting some action than their tongues' attempts at flattery.

Arthur tossed me the sword, and I caught the hilt in my right hand. I took a moment to admire its craftsmanship. They didn't make them like this anymore. From the corner of my eye, I saw a flash of steel. I raised the sword in my hand and met Arthur's blade.

"I forget how old you are," I said as steel met steel. "I don't want to be accused of abusing the elderly."

"I'm used to keeping my weapon up all night."

Our eyes connected. His steely gaze twinkled in challenge as mine darkened in acceptance. Now this was my kind of foreplay.

I'd flirted with kings in the past. I'd even batted my eyelashes at a Greek god or two. But never an Arthur. They'd always been married and deeply devoted to their women. This was the first unattached King of Camelot, and he was coming straight for me.

He struck out, lightning quick. I dodged the blow easily, resetting my stance. Arthur planted his massive thighs into the floor, facing me head-on. He was using a heavy broad sword. One-handed. Extending upward from his groin.

"Oh, Arthur," I said in my breathiest Marilyn Monroe voice. "Is that a sword in your armor or are you just happy to see me?"

He grinned. Then he released one of his hands from the hilt and made a come-hither motion at me. My grin spread as my grip tightened. I charged. When our blades connected, the force of my thrust knocked him back a foot.

"You don't speak like a woman in a committed relationship." He raised his sword over his head and brought it down. I blocked him with my blade, but his strength set my teeth rattling. I grunted and used nearly all of my strength to push the warrior back another foot.

"You don't move like a woman who has had a man recently either."

Here was the thing women needed to understand about a knight before climbing into the saddle with him or allowing him to climb up a balcony into her bedroom window: Knights were chivalrous to a fault. But that mostly pertained to witches. Any knight would lay down his life for a witch. Those kinds of women were sacred, holy beings in a knight's eyes.

But human women and Immortals were fair game.

"I just got out of a long relationship," I said.

Arthur advanced. He brought his sword up from down low.

I hopped out of the blade's path. "I'm kinda dating someone right now, though."

"Kinda?" Arthur whipped his blade in a figure-eight pattern that I matched and then stepped into to get a blow at his solar plexus. He grunted but kept coming, thrusting his dagger straight for my gut.

I turned my body to the side, barely missing the pointy tip. "It's in the beginning stages. Kinda."

"Kinda?" Arthur struck again. This time, our swords met with a loud crash. We both were breathing hard from the exertion.

"We were in a relationship before. But it didn't work out. We're trying again. Kinda," I said. "It's complicated."

"Relationships always are."

"Which is why you're a confirmed bachelor."

We were in a tight clench. The sharp edges of our swords made a slicing sound as we braced against each other, searching for dominance. He was close enough that I could extend my lips and test the whiskers of his beard to see if they were soft or prickly. We were close enough to kiss. Instead, we struck again with our swords.

"Not for long," he said. "I'm going to propose to Gwin."

"You're going to marry your brother's widow?"

I dropped my guard. Which was obviously a mistake in combat, but a huge mistake with this man. Arthur never let his guard slip.

He body-checked me as I'd done twice to him. The force of his blow sent me stumbling backward. I tucked and rolled, then came up in a low crouch, sword at the ready. A good thing, too, because he was on me the moment my head came up.

"But you don't love her," I said as I tucked and rolled again. This time when I stood, I was behind him. The move gave me only a split second before his broad sword swiped at my midsection. I felt the whisper of the blade on my belly button.

"I care for her," he said as he thrust toward my right side. I stepped into his movement and shoved the hilt of my sword into his side. He grunted and took a step back. "But more importantly, it's the right thing to do. She was groomed to be the lady of this castle." He thrust to my left side. "I need to produce an heir." He thrust to my left side again. "It's best for all." He aimed and thrust his sword straight for my heart, but his advance came up short.

"That is so romantic," I deadpanned.

"I'm Celtic, not Roman. We do what we must."

My sword had been extended, ready to make another pass, but now I recoiled. "No woman wants to be a *must*. We all want to be a *need*."

Arthur lowered his sword. "I don't understand the difference." His brow crinkled as he regarded me.

"Of course you don't."

I charged, not giving him a moment or an inch of mercy. Arthur gave as good as he got. The room filled with our grunts as we met iron with iron. The sounds of metal scratching and scraping filled the room along with the pounding of our feet as we thrust toward each other, dug in our heels to dig deeper, and then advanced again and again.

We came together a final time, giving the blows everything we had. Neither of us relented. We both collapsed to the floor, breathing hard.

"It's an honorable decision," he said after a few moments of catching his breath.

I gulped down a lungful of air before

responding. "You know she doesn't believe Merlin's dead?"

"I wish that were so, but it's been nearly three decades. He couldn't survive off the grid for that long. He wasn't the strongest man to begin with."

Arthur and Merlin were born half a century apart. That was like being a decade older than a sibling in normal human time. So, they weren't very close. Especially with Merlin sick in bed for most of his life. The current Arthur had grown up healthy and strong. He'd taken over many of his father's duties by the time Merlin had gained some strength with Gwin's help. But it didn't mean Arthur didn't care about his older brother.

"He should have never left the castle on his own," Arthur said.

"He wanted to be like his heroic brother."

"Heavy is the head that wears this crown." Arthur gave a humorless laugh, then he quickly sobered. "Merlin had been going on and on about hearing the voice of God. We thought it was the magic overwhelming him again."

I turned on my side and looked down at him. I'd always thought of Arthur as an overbearing overlord. But he looked like a man in this moment.

Just an ordinary man with a mountain of responsibility on his shoulders. I knew the feeling.

"Sometimes I feel that I'm failing," he said.

My eyes went wide, but he either didn't see or chose to ignore my shocked expression. His gaze stretched up to the ceiling. His arm was thrust over his head, and his chest rose and fell rapidly as though he'd just finished tumbling his lover and was now telling her his darkest secrets.

"I'm certain it was the Templars who got my brother. We never found his body. A witch and her family were murdered today. They lived out in a remote place, but somehow the Templars found them."

Arthur the Third had been a boy during the final witch hunts of the late 1800s. His grandfather had lost his life in earlier hunts. I knew the very thought of anything harming someone in his charge cut him to his core.

"Circe wasn't a powerful witch. She was nearing the end of her life. What kind of bastard would prey on a weak woman?"

He closed his eyes as his face scrunched in pain. It was such a human moment. I didn't know what to do for him. I'd never seen Arthur as human.

"We're stretched thin, and I'm trying to protect them all," he said. "There are those who are stubborn and won't come back to the castle where they can be protected until we root out the Templars. I don't have enough knights to station at every ley center. It's the Grail they're after—it has to be. They haven't been this active for hundreds of years. I can't let them get to the Grail. I need your help, Nia."

Arthur turned to me then. His eyes wide, his face unguarded just like his body that was splayed on the ground next to me. His most vulnerable parts were unprotected.

"You have it."

I was a sucker for threats of genocide. If someone was trying to eradicate an entire population, I was the first to raise my hand to stop it.

"Thank you," I said, hefting myself up to a sitting position and then coming to stand.

"For what?"

"I needed a good tumble."

"Anytime," he said, laughing.

Arthur's laugh sounded like a broken thing. But he took my outstretched hand and rose alongside me.

CHAPTER TEN

My eyes were a little blurry when Arthur and I stepped over the threshold of the armory. The sun had set and last meal would be served shortly. The great smells hit my nose, a low whistle hit my ears, and red hit my eyes.

Ginger-haired Lance came to a dead stop in the middle of the hall. He took in Arthur's bare, sweaty chest and the bruises darkening his skin. He took in my mussed hair and the slight swelling of my upper lip where Arthur had gotten me. They were such minor wounds to beings like us that would be completely healed within the hour. But I was sure the sight of it looked as though we'd been doing something other than sparring.

Lance arched an eyebrow at Arthur. The brow raise was loud and clear for *Dude, did you hit that?*

Arthur didn't even bother to correct his second-at-arm's thoughts. He rolled his eyes and headed in the opposite direction. I wasn't a witch, so my virtue needed no protection. I had to defend myself.

"It's not what you think," I said.

Lance rubbed his chin, a grin on his face. "I think he's getting some."

"Oh, he got something all right—a beat down."

"So you two were playing with his swords?"

I jerked my fist beside my head, ready to unload.

"I'm kidding." Lance held up his hands in surrender as he laughed. "Nice work on that blow to his gut, though."

I inclined my head at the compliment, preparing to head off to my rooms. I needed a shower before the meal. But Lance reached out and stayed me.

"Hey, I wanted to ask you something."

I waited patiently for him to speak again. Then waited a little less patiently a minute longer. By the second minute of him chewing at his lip and searching for words, I became entirely impatient.

"So you're single now?" he asked.

I looked up at the redheaded warrior. In that moment, he looked like a schoolboy trying to get up the courage to ask the popular girl out. Lance and I had flirted a couple of times over the decades. Harmlessly, though. I'd been in a committed relationship longer than he'd been alive.

"Yeah…" I said the single syllable slowly, stretching the word in two.

"How long did you wait until you jumped back into the saddle?"

My face contorted in absolute confusion. Saddle? Horseback riding?

A laugh trickled down the hall, and Lance's eyes shot up like a heat-seeking missile. I looked over my shoulder to see two blonde women coming down the stairway toward us. Gwin and Loren were engaged in conversation as they moved slowly, stopping every moment to talk animatedly. Gwin looked like the perfect miss next to Loren's bad girl. It was clear which woman was saddled with Lancelot's attentions. And his reference became clear.

"I waited six weeks," I said.

I wallowed for six weeks after breaking up with Zane before I considered dating Tres. I didn't tell Lance that I was still stutter-stepping my way toward the new horse in the race.

"I think twenty-five years is a long enough mourning period," I said.

"What?" Lance blinked and looked down at me. But only for a moment.

It was as though when Gwin was near, his eyes found her, like a magnet. And she was no better.

I saw her attention wasn't on Loren. She looked from the side of her eyes at Lance as Loren continued to chatter on.

"Maybe now's your chance," I said.

Lance opened his mouth, but no words came out. Then he brought his thumb to his lip and chewed at the nail. He hunched up his shoulders and let out a sigh. It was fascinating to witness. I'd watch this man smooth-talk his fair share of maidens and lightskirts. Yet when this single woman came anywhere near him, he turned into an untried youth.

"I always thought you and Gwin would wind up together. I was shocked when she married Merlin."

That snapped him out of his infatuated daze. "Merlin was a sycophant who took advantage of her kindness and good heart since the day she was born."

I had to listen close, as his Scottish brogue was a

thick layer on his tongue as he spoke ill of Gwin's departed husband and his leader's brother.

"God rest his soul," he tacked on begrudgingly.

"Oh, well tell me how you really feel."

He stared down at me in confusion. "She didn't love him. She pitied him. Her mother pushed the match, thinking she'd position her daughter to be the lady of the castle. And Gwin has always done what she thought was best for all. But she was nothing more than Merlin's sick nurse for most of his miserable life."

Lance looked up again. I knew the moment his gaze found her. His jaw unclenched. His eyes softened. His mouth went slack. This dude had it bad. But he wasn't making any move toward her.

"Lance, a word of advice. You'd better hurry up and tap that before another man swoops in."

But he wasn't paying attention to me anymore. Gwin and Loren were just feet away from us.

"Hey, Lancey," Loren said as she came up. "Have you heard the news? Gwin and I are cousins, which makes us family."

"What?" he said. "Oh no, no. Gwin and I aren't related. I mean, we're family because we're all one community here. But not by blood. Anyway, I need to…"

He took a step but bumped into Gwin.

"I'm so sorry," Gwin said.

"No, it's my fault, my lady."

He held onto her for a moment longer than prudent. Then the two seemed to realize they had an audience. Lance bowed and took off down the hall. Gwin watched him go. Loren and I looked at each other.

"I was just coming to check and make sure you had everything you need," Gwin said.

"I do," I said. "Do you?"

Her smile faltered. "I don't know what you mean."

"Gwin, I know what it is to hold on to someone when they're gone. But it's okay to move on."

"I do know that it's time to move on." Her gaze trailed down the hall as Lance turned the corner.

"Maybe it's time to get back out in the field," I said. "Merlin would've wanted you to be happy."

"I know what I must do," she said.

So it wasn't going to take divine intervention to get those two together. I patted her hand. "Good, and it's okay."

"I know that Arthur is going to propose."

I frowned, my palm stilling over her knuckles. I

felt the cold of the gold band from her first husband there. "You don't have to say yes."

"It is the sensible thing to do. It's Arthur's duty to continue the line, and I was meant to be the mother of the next in this great family."

Wow. Just...wow. "What does your heart tell you to do?"

Gwin stared at me in confusion. "I've never understood why people say that. My heart? My heart loves my people, my work. If I listen to my heart, I'll naturally do what's best for them. My head tells me to do the logical thing, which is the same duty. What I'm trying not to pay attention to are my loins."

If I had liquid in my mouth, I would've spit it out to hear such a thing come out of proper Gwin's mouth.

"I can't afford such irresponsibility. So, I'll do my duty. I'll see you both at last meal." And with that, Gwin took off down the hall in the opposite direction that her loins desired her to go.

"Dude, this place is full of pent-up sexual tension," Loren said. "No wonder my mother wanted to get out of here."

I turned and faced her. She looked the same, but somehow different. "So. You're a witch."

Loren snorted. "Did you have any doubt?"

"How do you feel?"

"Disappointed. I can't shoot any magic out of my hand or make things fly or brew a potion. I only have witch's blood with none of the power."

"But there are still perks," I said. "You could stay here and live a long life."

"Under a repressive dictator."

"It's just while there's danger. It wasn't always like this." Well, there was the Middle Ages. And then the Salem Witch Trials. And even now, there were some countries that still accused individuals of witchcraft and ostracized them, imprisoned them, and, in some cases, killed them. "But this is your family."

"You're my family."

I didn't let on how much that warmed my heart, but the gush of the breath I'd been holding gave me away.

"Let's take care of this mission first," Loren said. "Then we'll figure out the rest."

She looped arms with me as I'd seen her do with Gwin as they'd strolled and chatted. We walked in a companionable silence for a few steps before she said what was on her mind.

"So," Loren said. "There's definitely some sexual tension between you and Arthur. This isn't exactly a yacht, but a girl could get used to a castle."

"There's tension between Arthur and me, but it isn't sexual."

It had never been sexual. We danced around each other and flirted with our swords. But I thought if I showed him my boobs, he might be more interested in discussing their battle-ready properties than caressing either of them.

"You never hit that?" Loren asked.

"With my lady parts? No. With a blade—yeah. Once or twice."

"I think we need to have a talk about the birds and the bees, hon."

CHAPTER ELEVEN

I stood under the spray of the shower and let the grime of travel and the sweat of my battle with Arthur wash away from me. It wasn't the water that helped to clear my mind. It seemed I'd needed someone to knock some sense into me.

The bruises Arthur had delivered throbbed, but the sensation ebbed as things became clearer for me. I thought of Arthur, all alone with his duties. I thought of Gwin, unfulfilled in hers. And I thought of Lance, pining away while keeping his desires to himself.

I had no intention of going out like that. I didn't want to be alone. I didn't want to live an unsatisfied life. I didn't want to yearn for someone who didn't choose me above all others.

I wrapped a towel around myself and stepped out of the bathroom. My phone sat on the bed. I sat down on the mattress and pulled the device to myself. There were no missed calls or texts. I checked my email and saw that there was a job from the IAC. I'd deal with that later.

I pulled up my contacts list. Zane was my top favorite. Had been ever since I'd gotten my very first cell phone. That original device had been a brick in my hand and it almost never connected us, but it was a lifeline while we were separated.

I hovered over the delete key but couldn't bring myself to press it. It would've been an empty gesture anyway. The sequence of numbers that would connect me to him was one of the few things that was burned into my memory.

I pulled up another contact. This one I didn't know by heart. I didn't plan to hover too long over Tresor Mohandis's phone number. It was time to move on.

I took a moment to plan what I'd say. I ran vocal tone options through my head.

Seductive? No, not yet. We'd only been on two dates. And one of those dates didn't count since a dead body had been involved.

Professional? No. That would inevitably lead to a

fight. If there was a hint of his business as a land developer and my business as a tree-hugging tomb-saver, we'd be at each other's throats. And not in the good way.

Friendly? Probably not a good idea since I wasn't trying to stay too long in the friend zone. Even though we'd only been there for a couple of months.

What was left? I ticked the options off on my fingers—seductive, professional, friendly. Was there any other way to speak to a man?

My finger slipped as I was pondering and hit the *call* button. I didn't have time to think. It was answered on the first ring.

"This is Tresor Mohandis's phone," said a woman with a husky voice. "How may I help you?"

In the split second I'd had to plan, I'd decided to wing it and simply say hello. But the single word caught in my throat. The woman who answered Tres's phone didn't sound professional or friendly. Her tone dropped low into the register of seduction. I also heard a cat-like note of smirk.

I cleared my throat. "I'm sorry, I thought this was Mr. Mohandis's personal line."

"It is."

And then silence. But the silence felt like a challenge. The adrenaline I'd burned facing off against Arthur shot through my veins.

Unfortunately for this chick, I healed fast. I cracked the bones in my neck and sat up straight, the soreness gone from my back. My busted lip was ready to take on a fight through the receiver.

"Well, is he there?" I demanded.

"I'm sorry. He's occupied at the moment." Her voice dripped saccharine and burned a hole through the line. "But I can take a message."

"Well, this is his..." His what? I wasn't his girlfriend. I wasn't exactly his ex-lover, at least not in this century. "Tell him it's Theta. He'll want to talk to me."

"Oh," she cooed. "They all say that, sweetie."

I reared back from the phone receiver, wishing I could reach through and wring this woman's neck.

"I'll just leave your name on the pile of others."

I hung up the phone, smashing the *end* button repeatedly with my thumb. And then got pissed at myself because that was obviously what she'd been goading me to do. But I didn't dare call back. I'd been humiliated enough for now.

I should've known better. Tresor Mohandis was a renowned playboy. He had women at his feet, including the ones who answered his personal phone. He might not have been sleeping with the saccharine phone operator, but he had handed her his phone. The line he'd given me to call him direct. Probably because he was done with me.

He'd been so preoccupied with my relationship with Zane, insisting my old boyfriend always came between us. And now that Zane and I were well and truly over, where was Tres? He'd probably just enjoyed the chase, and now that I was caught, he was on to the next challenge.

Maybe Arthur, Gwin, and Lance had it right. I should just focus on my duties, my work. My work never failed to make me happy—except when it was trying to kill me.

I tossed the phone aside. Rummaging through my bag, I finally pulled on a pair of jeans and a cotton top. Then I ran a hand through my unruly hair, headed for the door, and opened it.

Loren stood on the other side with her arm raised as though she was prepared to knock. She looked flushed in the face and happy. Like she belonged here.

"I'm surprised you're here," I huffed. "I figured you'd forgotten me."

She frowned. "What's got your panties in a bunch?"

"You've been hanging out with everyone but me."

That wasn't true. She'd just left me twenty minutes ago to shower.

"Oh," she cooed, wrapping her arms around me and resting her cheek against my shoulder. "Is poor Nia feeling left out?"

I shrugged, but she didn't let go. Finally, I relented. When I spoke my irritation into her shoulder, the words came out muffled.

"Some stupid woman answered Tres's phone."

"What?" Loren reared back. "He's cheating on us? I'll kill him."

Loren considered my relationship with the yacht-owning, private-jet-hopping billionaire real estate developer a family affair. Even though she and Zane got along really well, she was Team Broody Billionaire.

Zane was an artist and far from a starving one. He simply had little interest in wealth or material things. Whereas Tres set about possessing anything, and it would appear everyone, that came within his purview.

"No need," I said. "I'm done with men. I'm going to focus solely on my work."

"Oh. Cool. Another sabbatical from males. This time in a castle full of virile knights. Yay."

We took off in the direction of the dining hall.

When we entered, everyone was already seated. Arthur and his knights sat at a table near the doors, likely a strategic position. Though Camelot had never been breached, the knights were ever ready.

The townsfolk and their families were spread out around the other tables. There wasn't an empty table in the hall for Loren and me to claim. I'd never been to high school, but I'd seen the movies, read the books, and heard tons of accounts of the angst that came with the school cafeteria. Sweat beaded at my neck as I tried to determine where I might fit in.

"Well," Loren said, "come on. You can come sit at the cool kids' table. I'll give you an in."

"Wherever I sit is the cool kids' table."

"That's my girl."

Loren grabbed my hand and tugged me toward a table near Arthur and his knights. Gwin and Morgan scooted over and made space for us. Food was shoved in front of me, and I lost myself in the good tastes for a moment.

Loren barely touched her meal as she chatted with every person at our table and the nearby ones. I was usually a social butterfly, but Loren looked like she belonged here. Because she did. This was her family.

"Listen, Loren, about the mission tonight?"

"Hmm? Oh, I'm ready."

"I was thinking maybe you stay back."

She frowned at me. "If I do, who's going to have your back?"

I wanted to hug her. But even more, I wanted her to be here to hug when this mission was over. "You just found your family."

"I don't know these people. I want to. But we're doing that whole butt-sniffing thing people do when meeting a new potential pack member. And I'm sure there'll be hoops that I have to jump through for everyone to accept me. You and me, we've already sniffed each other's butts and run the gamut. I'm still rolling with you."

She gave me a shoulder bump and then picked up a turkey leg. But she paused before it met her mouth.

"Or," she said, "I mean, if you're dead set against me going on this little adventure, I could stay behind in an unguarded castle filled with priceless magical artifacts."

Loren dropped the bone and rubbed her crafty fingers together like a villain. I laughed. Beside us, Morgan took in an incredulous gasp. She whipped her body around to face the table behind us where the knights sat, including Arthur.

"Wait! What? She's going?" Morgan pointed a finger at Loren, but she glared at Arthur. "But she's a witch."

Arthur raised a lazy gaze to Loren. Then he sat back in his chair and really studied her. Now that she'd been declared of a magical bloodline, he might have a say in her movements.

I put a possessive arm around Loren. "She's with me. She hasn't accepted your dominion."

Loren leaned into me. "Um, Nia, hang on. That sounds"—she cocked her head and studied Arthur—"interesting. What exactly does it mean to be under a knightly king's dominion?"

"It means," Morgan said through clenched teeth, "that you have to do what he says, even if it's stupid, sexist, and archaic. Like delay your acceptance to university because it's a *dangerous time for magical kind.*" Her voice went into a deep register, likely to mimic Arthur's voice. But it sounded childish coming from her.

Loren took a deep breath and pinched her eyebrows. She leaned even closer to me and stage-whispered, "I'm assuming she means outside the bedroom?"

I nodded.

Arthur quirked a brow.

Morgan gagged.

Loren shrugged, her hands facing upward in a placating fashion. "Then sorry, no. That's against my religion. I believe the only place a man should rule is in the bedroom."

Morgan looked between the two. She turned around in her seat to fully face Arthur. "Then I reject your dominion, too. On religious grounds."

Arthur breathed in through his nose and then out his mouth. "You can't," he said to Morgan. Then he inclined his head toward Loren. "She can. She's more human than witch. She doesn't need my protection."

Morgan stomped her foot under the table, but it resonated. "I'm a witch, not some delicate flower."

"I fail to understand the difference," Arthur deadpanned, turning back to his plate.

"You can't keep me caged in this castle, you fascist."

"Morgan, do you even know what a fascist is?" Arthur sliced the meat from his bone in tiny bites while Morgan seethed.

"Of course I do. I have two advanced degrees. But you wouldn't know that."

Arthur plopped the slice of meat into his mouth and chewed. His face was a study of unconcern. I thought Morgan would blow a gasket, but instead she changed tactics.

"At least let me be of use if I have to stay caged here. Let me go with you."

"Out of the question," Arthur said around his bite of food.

All around us, the conversation continued. People largely ignored this fight as though it happened on a regular basis.

"How are you going to get past the humans at the tunnel?" Morgan asked.

"That's not for you to worry about." He took another bite of the small cut.

"I can place an enchantment over you, a shield to hide you from human view. Like the enchantment Gwin and I cast over the town. You'll be able to slip in easily with my help. If you won't let me go to grad school, then at least let me be useful while I'm here."

Arthur slowly pulled the tines of the fork from his mouth. "No."

"You know," I said, "being shielded from view would actually make it easier and safer to slip in." Then I shut up when Arthur glared daggers at me.

"I would stay at a safe distance," Morgan hedged. "Just because you lost your brother doesn't mean you can cage all of us."

Conversation did stop then. Gwin froze like a statue beside me. The knights looked at one another and then at their leader from the corner of their eyes. Arthur's throat worked. Then he reached for his goblet and took two gulps. Finally, the silence was broken by loud footsteps coming closer.

A dark figure entered the doorway. All eyes went to him. The man looked like a Samurai warrior misplaced in medieval England. I knew that Gawain's father had gone on a quest in Japan a few hundred years ago. He'd come back with a treasure for the court and a treasure of his own whom he made his wife.

Gawain arched a dark brow as he regarded the room. Even as his eye lowered, his brow looked as though it remained arched. His dark hair curled around his honey-golden skin, the tendrils caressing his face. His dusky eyes looked stormy as they skated over me, and his lip quirked. Then his gaze fastened on Loren.

"Holy hotness on a stick," Loren breathed.

Gawain's grin told me that he'd heard her and the appreciation was mutual. Sir Gawain was hot, but holy he wasn't. He winked at Loren before turning to his lord and commander.

"What news?" Arthur asked.

"The camera crews are gone from the entrance to the site," Gawain reported. His deep voice rumbled through the hall.

Morgan scowled. Her only in on the mission was thwarted.

"But a crew of archaeologists remain," said Gawain.

"Oh, I can help with that," I said.

Both men turned to me.

"How?" Arthur asked.

"I have credentials."

CHAPTER TWELVE

We headed to the stables under the full moon's light. The steeds in the stalls were magnificent beasts. The horses were all Arabians, the oldest breed known to the world. The breed, which hailed from the deserts of the Middle East, were prized for their speed, endurance, and strong bones. I had no idea how these horses came to be in the employ of a group of knights from medieval times where heavy armor was the prized battle tactic. But the real Knights of the Round Table had never bothered much with heavy armor, having magical swords and shields to protect them from their foes.

Arthur, Lance, and Gawain strode into the stables. Each wore leather breeches that hugged at their powerful thighs. Their defined chests were covered with loose tunics. The knights pulled chain mail shirts over their heads. The metal was lightweight and embedded with magic. Nothing but a magical sword would get through it.

Arthur pulled out a saddle and placed it on a mare for me. I knew this mare. Rather, I knew her mother. She'd been born the last time I was here. She came up to my hand and nuzzled my palm, whispering a greeting into my mind and offering me her services.

"Whoa," Loren said. "That was trippy. It sounded like my horse just said hello."

"He did," I assured her.

People weren't the only beings that the ley lines blessed with magic. But sometimes, the translation between magical beasts and people went a little wonky.

"It sounded like he said welcome back," Loren said as she nuzzled the horse's nose. "But I've never been here."

"Maybe he thinks you're your mother?"

Broad shoulders blocked the entry beside me, shutting out the moon. Gawain's wicked lips curled as he held out a saddle for Loren.

"This horse is from the line of Sir Galahad's first

mare," Gawain said. Then he asked Loren, "Do you ride?"

Loren bit her lip, not out of shyness. There wasn't a shy bone in Loren's body. "Give me a leg up?"

Loren extended her leg, making both her words and her actions suggestive.

Gawain took her calf in hand and then slid his big palm down to her heel. I should have warned her about this particular knight back in the dining hall when they'd caught each other's eye.

Gawain was notorious for loving them and leaving them. He couldn't hang around even if he wanted to. He had a curse on his head. One day he'd have to face death—literally.

But then again, ever since I'd known Loren, she'd had no problem loving and leaving men. Maybe it was Gawain I should warn. Or better yet, I'd keep out of whatever was brewing between those two and get my own love life in order.

Arthur mounted his steed alongside Lance. The five of us took off into the night. The horses' hooves beat a steady rhythm, bringing us closer to the caves.

I hadn't ridden in a while, at least not at a full gallop. Definitely not at the speed of a magical steed, which approached seventy miles per hour. I held on tight to the reins as the horse's speed defied logic. It felt like we were flying.

A memory shook loose in my mind. I was airborne, falling, flying, running through a... garden. Up above me, the leaves were a deep purple that I couldn't remember ever seeing before. The flowers were such a lush pink that defied hue, tone, and saturation.

And the smell? Even in my mind's eye, every gulp of air tasted like the sweetest dessert. Behind me I saw my friend Vau walking hand in hand with her paramour Epsilon. Aleph sat in the field picking flowers, Yod watched her from a distance as he stood beside Bet. On the far side, I saw Delta huddled with Zeta and Evan. The ever-reclusive Ian sat beneath a tree alone. Up ahead, Tres and Zane stood close together...laughing.

What the hell?

I blinked, bringing myself back to the present. Deep in my heart of hearts, I knew that wasn't a vision. It was a memory. One I'd never had before. One I'd never dreamed possible. All twelve Immortals together. I felt myself being pulled somewhere familiar, somewhere I'd forgotten.

You will be allowed to return soon. Igraine's prophetic words echoed in my head as the winds slapped my forehead. More and more, they were seeming less prophecy and more prediction. Or better yet, a forecast. Unlike the storm that had brought me here to Caerleon, it didn't feel like everyone would make it out alive.

The horse slowed to a trot as we reached the top of the hill. Down below, I heard the gentle crashing of waves. Up ahead, I saw familiar lights. They were floodlights, the type used at a night dig. I also recognized several remote sensing devices that would be used as the archeologist on site tried to see what was below the ground before actually digging it up or descending.

Gawain had been right. The camera crews with their spotlights were gone. But the archaeologists weren't the only light source or organized group around.

A group of people, some dressed in flowing robes, others in strips of fabric and headdresses, danced and chanted around a fire. Wiccans.

The knights looked on in disgust as the barely clad women danced around a man with a pointed hat singing praises to the earth and moon. I'd met many witches throughout my long life. I'd met my fair share of pagans as well.

A witch was born just like any human. Who that

witch or human became after birth was a series of decisions. A witch or human could make choices that led them to either the dark side of the force or the light side of the force.

The dark side might include forcing others to do things against their will, murder, and forming a boy band. There were other choices, too, like deciding on a career, a spouse, a political party, and a religion.

Wicca and paganism were religions. I didn't believe that all religions were bad. Just like I didn't believe that all careers or politics were bad. It was what a person—human, witch, or other—chose to do with them.

I'd had run-ins with this particular branch of Wiccans before. They weren't bad people, but I didn't agree with their decision-making process. Exhibit A—ritual sex.

I wasn't a prude. But when there are more women than men present in a religion that has ritual sex as a tenant, I get suspicious.

The chanting man stopped his unintelligible diatribe and reached out for a woman. He locked lips with her and then reached for another, repeating the process as the other women continued to twirl their torsos and swivel their hips in anticipation.

Witches had been persecuted for thousands of years. In the Middle Ages alone, nearly fifty thousand men and women lost their lives for being accused of practicing dark arts. Very few of them actually had magical blood. What these people in present day were doing by gyrating under the moon was a mockery of everything these knights fought to protect.

I came up to Arthur. Placing a hand on his bicep, I felt nothing but tension. "We have a mission to complete. Let's hurry inside."

I watched his throat work before he glanced down at me. Then he turned and led the way toward the entrance. I stepped in front of him as we approached the cordoned-off area.

The area was entirely unassuming. I could understand how it could have been overlooked for centuries. Whoever had chosen this spot had done well. It was in plain sight and completely hidden at the same time.

"There's more activity than we expected," Lance said.

"Let me handle this," I said, approaching a middle-aged man with a notepad in his hands. "Dr. Nia Rivers, IAC." I presented him with my identification card.

The man narrowed his gaze, scrutinizing the card. Then he cursed. "You IAC bastards, always trying to get in on a dig."

"I'm just here to take a look."

"That's what the other guy said."

"Other guy?" I said.

"He's already down there."

I looked over my shoulder at Arthur. The IAC didn't move this fast. It was a bureaucratic organization, and it would take weeks to cut through the red tape to get access to this find. Whoever was down there wasn't official.

Arthur shouldered past the other man and made his way down the makeshift stairway. They'd widened the rabbit hole to make a man-sized entrance. Down, down, down we went. The air got thinner and danker with each step until the light from above was a distant memory.

Arthur held up a charm that lit the way, illuminating the dark cave to show off the nooks and crevices. And just like that, the archaeologist in me turned on full blast.

The walls were damp as we went further down. I tasted salt in the air. The thing about underground caves was they preserved things so well because of the humidity. As we stepped down on solid ground, I saw there were tunnels that snaked out in three different directions. Each passage was cast in dark shadows, giving no hint of what hid in its depths. But above the entryways were scratches in the rock.

"Which way do we go?" Arthur asked.

I looked at the writings on the walls above the tunnels. Only two had any markings. Over one, I saw the cross symbol. It could've been for the crucifix, or for Christ. But I assumed it was the symbol for the Knights Templar.

Over the second tunnel, there was a symbol for witch. Arthur recognized it too. We headed in the direction of the witch.

The entry was tight around my body. It had to be cramped for the three knights. But we made our way through. When we entered the chamber, I immediately wished we'd gone the other way.

If the wanna-be witches above us could see these atrocities, they'd pull on jeans and sweatshirts and head inside a Puritan church where it was safe.

There were rusted manacles on the walls held up by chains. Small cuffs for the wrists. Wider cuffs hanging high for the neck. Cuffs hanging lower for the torso.

An array of bones littered the floor, brushed haphazardly into corners, and piled in a shallow pit.

Tattered pieces of rope still clung to some of the bones as though the bodies had simply been cut down and tossed in what was likely a fire pit, the singed rope still dangling from the deceased's necks. Faint traces of red still stained the stone walls and floors.

This had been a torture chamber for witches.

All around me, the knights breathed in shallow pants as though they could feel the pain of the witches who'd been tortured and murdered in here. The room was heavy with the knights' sorrow, anger, and helplessness. These had been actual witches, not humans accused of power they didn't have. I knew because I could still feel a faint trace of power in the air.

Gwin had said the only way for magic to die was to burn the body of the witch or wizard who had contained it. I supposed that would explain the char marks on the bones and the pile of dust in the corner. But the residual effects of the power were still present in the dust.

I reached for the comfort of my dagger at my hip. I'd traded it for one of my sai swords, bringing the big guns tonight, just in case. And boy, this was a case.

I spied small pots, bowls, and a cup in the corner.

I left the knights to their commiseration and approached the cup. It lay on its side, as though it had been used and discarded. It couldn't be this simple.

"Is that it?" I turned to Arthur.

He blinked as though he didn't know what I meant. Then he turned away from me and shook his head. "He wouldn't have left the Grail on English soil."

"He who?" I asked. "Wait, what? So, you knew the Grail wasn't in here?"

"We're looking for a clue to its location. Likely in an ancient script. Perhaps on the walls, or maybe on a piece of parchment."

I shook my head at him. First, he'd said the Grail hadn't been in the knights' possession for centuries. Now, the place where he believed it might be would only offer up a clue? Was he leading me on a wild goose chase? And if so, to what end?

I took a step toward Arthur and heard the crunch of bone. I looked down at the body I'd desecrated. I set my mouth to apologize to the deceased when I saw that the corpse was swathed in the tunic of a Templar, the red cross preserved in the humid room.

In the Middle Ages, the Knights Templar wore white tunics with a red cross on the chest. The cross was a symbol of martyrdom. To die in combat was considered a great honor. But this man had died in a hole where he'd once tortured the innocent.

Looking closer, I noted that he was remarkably well preserved for someone who had died at least five hundred years ago. Decomposition was slowest underground. A body lying directly in soil without a coffin could take up to twelve years to decay into bone. After half a millennium, there was still skin on this man's bones.

"Is that him?" Lance asked.

Arthur moved around me and bent over the corpse. After a brief investigation, he nodded and then began to search the dead man's pockets.

"What the hell?" I said. "You can't do that."

Arthur spared me a glance.

"Those bones are an ancient artifact. Would you at least use gloves?"

"Says the woman who just stepped on his neck."

Ignoring Arthur, I reached into my sack. I pulled out and handed him a pair of protective gloves.

He looked at the proffered gloves, then back to me, and finally back down to the corpse. Giving me a dismissive glare, he reached beneath the tunic and began rummaging around.

"Is magic transferable?" I asked, giving up and

looking around at the remains of the dead witches. "Otherwise, how is it that this Templar is so well preserved?"

No one answered. In fact, I felt a marked tension in the room at my question. I looked up at Lance and Gawain only to see that they were studiously avoiding my gaze.

Arthur pulled out an ancient sheet of parchment, a scroll. "This must be it."

"That must be what?" I asked.

Arthur straightened and handed the ancient parchment to me. I reached out my hand and then pulled back to put on the gloves. Arthur huffed with impatience, but I ignored him. My misstep had been a mistake. He could destroy history if he wanted to, but I wouldn't be a part of the destruction.

Once the gloves were on, Arthur shoved the paper in my hand. "Can you read this?"

"What exactly is this?" I asked, taking the paper gingerly. "A suicide note?"

No one answered.

"Who was that man?" I said.

"A traitor to our kind," Arthur said grimly.

I took a better look at the document, hoping it would be something as simple as a map. I was good at following directions, putting one foot in front of the other. But there was writing on this document and not images.

"Can you read it?" he asked. "Do you know the language?"

"I know every language, and I can decipher any written symbol," I said. "Except for riddles."

"She hates riddles," Loren offered.

"I love them."

We all turned toward the sound of the intruder's voice. A tall man stood in the doorway. He wore a tunic much like the deceased knight's. The red cross was over his chest, but instead of white, it lay in a sea of black fabric.

"Father Gerard?" Loren asked in surprise.

"Hello, Ms. Van Alst. You're a vision, as ever." Father Gerard stood in the doorway with a group of men at his back. The men had swords drawn.

"Templars," Arthur growled.

CHAPTER THIRTEEN

"I'll take that scroll, if you don't mind," Father Gerard said.

"You're one of the bad guys?" Loren huffed. "How come I always fall for the villains?"

Her eyes connected with Gawain. She did a quick glance up and down his rock-hard body. Then she shrugged as though in acceptance of her perpetual plight.

"I'm not the bad guy, angel," Father Gerard said. He held a torch to light the way. "Magic, be it encased in an idol object or the veins of a human, is a scourge."

"Oh." Loren quirked her lip in a smirk. "I should probably tell you. I'm no angel. My mother was a witch."

Father Gerard didn't blink. He didn't narrow his eyes. His pupils didn't dilate as he looked at her with fresh eyes. Still, the light that had been in his eyes every time he'd glanced at Loren on the yacht dimmed. It turned into something dark. It was like watching the bright scales be sheared from a fish, leaving behind flesh and bones.

"I may not be on a first-name basis with God," Loren continued, "and I may not follow all the commandments, but I do know the one about 'love thy neighbor.'" She leaned into me. "That's one of them, right?"

"Yeah," I said. "But I think both you and the Father may have taken it to the extreme."

Loren had loved many a male neighbor, biblically. If Father Gerard was rolling with this new breed of the Knights Templar, then he was on the other end of the spectrum with killing anyone outside of his comfort zone.

Father Gerard took a deep breath and let it out slowly. He shook his head. "Magic is a disease. Luckily, I know the cure. I'm here to save your soul from these devils."

Gawain stepped in front of Loren. "Have you actually met the devil? 'Cause I have. A self-righteous, pompous arse like yourself would get along quite well with him."

"It's not too late for you to be saved." Father Gerard ignored everyone but Loren. Behind him, the Templars raised their swords in the shadows of the torch and the dim light of Arthur's charm.

"Keep your prayers, Father." Lance stepped up beside Gawain, sword raised. "No one's getting saved here tonight."

The Templars behind Father Gerard rustled, gripping their hilts and digging in their heels. But Father Gerard held out his free hand. "Can't we for once do this without violence? Just hand over our brother's scroll. Come with us willingly. And then you can make your peace with our Lord."

"You call for peace?" Arthur swaggered to the front of the defensive line. His sword swung by his thigh, his gait reminding me of the horses we'd rode here. "Yet you kill women and children."

Father Gerard shook his head. "No, not women and children. The demons that possessed them. You must understand that there is evil living inside of you, like a parasite. When it overtakes your spirit, it turns your eyes white. I've seen it happen."

Wait? White eyes? Oh. He had to be talking about a Chosen, the humans who shared their souls with one of the six Greek gods. When that energy transfer happened, the humans' souls were sucked out of their eyes, leaving them entirely white.

"My own mother was possessed. The devil made her do heinous acts that no child should ever witness. Sexual orgies with other lost and demoralized souls."

Heinous acts? Sex orgies with the devil? I got the feeling Father Gerard may have witnessed his mother at one of the Greek god Zeus's orgies. I'd witnessed one myself a while back, and the acts going on had made me blush.

But I felt that if the idea of witches and wizards upset the holy man so much, the idea of six gods and goddesses would set him off. So I remained mute.

The knights did as well. Without another word, Arthur lifted his sword and charged. But Father Gerard was swallowed by the advancing Templars.

I palmed my sword in one hand. In the other, which remained gloved, I held the scroll. But the knights formed a wall around me and Loren, keeping us bodily from the fight as they went toe to toe with the Templars.

"Are we just supposed to stand here like damsels?" Loren asked.

I watched the swordplay before us. Arthur,

Lance, and Gawain were outmanned, but they weren't outmatched.

A Templar advanced. He swung wide, and his sword knocked over one of the vases. It crashed to the floor.

I gasped.

"Ruh-roh," Loren said, sounding entirely too happy. "You just pissed off an archaeologist."

I stepped in front of Lance and sliced off the guy's hand. The Templar wailed, clutching the wrist of his severed hand. He slumped down at Father Gerard's feet.

Father Gerard looked from the man to Lance. His soulful eyes went dark as his face contorted into a sneer of hatred. He reached into his robes and pulled out a gem, a bluestone.

The stone looked similar to the one Arthur had used to light our way. But instead of light, this stone sent out a pulse of energy. I felt it brush past me like a strong gust of wind. It made me take a step back. It brought the knights to their knees. It knocked Loren off her feet.

Many thought that Stonehenge, and the other stone monuments like it around the world, was a celestial clock. It wasn't. Those large sarsen stones weren't arranged to track the passing of the seasons.

Each of the twenty-five ton, nine-meters tall stones weren't the focal point of the arrangement. The point had been the much smaller, rarer bluestones. A bluestone was like kryptonite to a witch or wizard.

Luckily, Arthur and his knights were more warrior than wizard. So the stones only knocked their breath out of them. Along with Loren, who also only had a touch of witch in her blood, they were quickly recovering.

I stepped up in the meantime. There were still three Templars standing alongside Father Gerard. Five more filled the doorway. The three up front advanced on Arthur, Lance, and Gawain.

I raised my sword high, ready to take on all three. The men stopped when they saw me and stared. Then they looked at one another.

Really? Again with the chivalry nonsense? Was I gonna get any action tonight?

Didn't look like it. Arthur and his knights ran past me. The Templar who faced off with Lance got in a blow to Lance's arm before Lance could run him through with his sword.

Gawain didn't fare much better. His sword had been knocked out of his hand with the blast. The Templar facing him got his blade up under the chain mail and into Gawain's side before Lance was able to come to his aid.

Arthur had also lost his sword, but that fact did not benefit the Templar who came at him. With just his brute strength, Arthur slammed his shoulder into the man and dropped him to the floor. I was certain I heard the man's skull crack as he hit the floor.

Arthur didn't spare the downed man a moment. He charged next for Father Gerard. With one blow, Arthur knocked the charm out of the holy man's hand. Then he put his large hand around Father Gerard's collarless neck. He put the Father between us and his knights and the Templars who were itching to get into the room from the entryway.

At the sight of their leader being at the mercy of the great Arthur, the Templars hesitated. But only for a second. It appeared they weren't an all-for-one-and-one-for-all kind of band. They inched into the room, swords drawn.

Arthur used his booted foot to kick up Excalibur and then he backed up, keeping his grip around Father Gerard's throat.

"You can't win," croaked Father Gerard. "We have God on our side."

"Whatever side you think you're standing on," Arthur said, "that can't be God at your back."

We continued to back up as the Templars advanced. They were pushing us further into the back of the room where there was no escape, only a wall.

The smell of salt thickened the air, as did the humidity. I hit the wall with a thump. But the thump sounded hollow. There were no hollow spots in caves. Unless...

I turned my back to the wall. "Please be a secret door. Please be a secret door."

I pressed every crevice I could find until I heard a creak, then pushed at the false rock with my shoulder. And finally, the door opened. The sounds of waves crashed into my ears. Salt danced on the tip of my tongue.

"Jump," Arthur shouted.

The waters below looked treacherous. But even more, the waters were wet and I held a precious, delicate ancient scroll in my hand. Even the air was anathema to it.

"Trust me," Arthur yelled. "Jump."

I did.

Instead of slamming into a wall of water as I expected, I landed in a cushion of air. There was water all around me, but I was mostly dry. I looked beside me to see Loren looking around in wonder as well.

One by one, the knights joined us in our bubble fortress.

Up above, the Templars stood at the edge of the cliff. The waters rose high as a tidal wave came and pushed them back in.

When the waters receded from the cave, I turned to see a woman floating in front of us. She was dressed in a crisp white nightgown. Her white hair billowed out around her. She looked like what I'd imagined I'd seen when we were at sea.

The ghostly-pale woman looked me up and down in that way one woman sizes up the next. But she was blatant about it. Her glances weren't covert.

"Viviane," Arthur said. "Get us back to the castle."

Viviane glared at Arthur. Then I noted on second glance that it wasn't Arthur she glared at, but Father Gerard, who was still held in Arthur's grip. Viviane clenched her teeth with distaste, but she did as Arthur bade.

She dove down into the waters. I expected to see fins. Instead, there were small feet beneath the flowing gown.

The bubble was pulled deep into the waters behind her. We were blinded by a harsh, glaring light. And then darkness.

"What's happening?" I shouted into the darkness.

"Relax." Lance's voice sounded disembodied. "The water is on the ley line. Every ley line across the world is connected, and we're able to travel from place to place along them with a witch's spell."

"So this is like a wormhole?" I asked.

"On an intraplanetary scale, yes."

"Viviane?" Loren mused. "Isn't that the name of the Lady in the Lake? Oh my god, she's real. My mother used to tell me stories about her."

"She was born with deformed legs," Lance said. His voice was strained in the darkness. I wondered how bad his wounds from the battle were. "When her human father saw her deformity, he threw her in the lake. Luckily, she was also born a witch. So she survived."

"It was her the other day," I said. "She made a storm in the sea." I knew that freak storm was supernatural. I imagined she'd been trying to keep Father Gerard away from this land. And now Arthur had foiled her attempts as she brought us into Camelot.

We surfaced in the mote surrounding the castle. The bubble burst and cool night air sailed into my lungs. We stepped out of the bubble and onto dry land.

"Thank you," I said to Viviane.

She eyed me with uncertainty. Then she turned to Loren. "You dropped this." She handed Loren her cane.

"My father's sword," Loren exclaimed, reaching down for her prized possession.

"No," Viviane said. "It was your mother's. Technically, it was her father's, Sir Galahad's. But he left it to her when he died." And then Viviane disappeared into the waters.

CHAPTER FOURTEEN

We left the moat and headed through the castle gates. Over the horizon, I could see the horses returning across the hills toward the stables. I had no idea how they knew we'd returned another way. I didn't understand everything magical.

We rushed the injured men inside the throne room. Morgan and Gwin were at our heels. Gwin looked at the severely injured Gawain and the less injured Lance. Indecision was clear on her face.

"Tend to him," Lance said.

"It's not like I'll die anytime soon," Gawain muttered. He choked when he tried to laugh off the pain. As he did, the wound in his side wept.

With one final, longing look at Lance, Gwin went to Gawain.

"What happened?" Morgan demanded.

"Help your sister," Arthur commanded. He tossed Father Gerard into one of the seats set apart from the Round Table. The other knights and a handful of elders were already assembled in the room.

"I'm not a nursemaid," Morgan said hotly.

Arthur slammed his sword into a holster and rounded on Morgan, tension in his every step. Luckily, the girl was smart, and she took a step back instead of standing her ground.

"You want to be a soldier?" Arthur growled.

Morgan gulped. When she spoke, it was a squeak. "Yes. I can wield a sword."

"And if the man by your side fell as the enemy advanced, what would you do?"

Morgan hesitated.

"Do you keep fighting? Or do you get him to safety to save his life?"

Morgan clenched her jaw, then she let the words tumble out. "I do what I must to save his life."

"We are in the fight of our lives, Morgan, and we are not winning. This is about more than you, more than your wishes, more than your desires. There is a man down."

The two stared each other off. Morgan's chin was lowered now, but her eyes were still steel. Arthur needed to say no more, his point was made. Morgan turned and joined her sister to look after Lance.

Arthur advanced on Father Gerard. The man scooted back in his chair as the large mass that was Arthur came toe to toe with him.

"You're a priest?" Arthur demanded.

"I am a soldier of God," Father Gerard said stiffly.

"Then we speak the same language. Who's your leader?"

"I told you—"

Arthur held up his index finger. "The mortal man. What's his name?"

"I do not serve any man or a false prophet such as yourself," said Father Gerard.

Arthur's proud chin tilted high. "I follow the words of our Lord, Jesus Christ, who teaches that *blessed are you when people insult you, persecute you, and falsely say all kinds of evil against you because of me.*"

Father Gerard scoffed. "I was told that your brother said the same thing before he was baptized by our savior."

Up until that moment, Arthur had been cool. His face had been an implacable wall of calm calculation. With the mention of his brother, I saw something snap in his eyes. His elders Sir Kay and Sir Bedivere came from the corners of the room, each laying a hand on his shoulders. Arthur's chest heaved as he tried to master himself. His hands clenched into fists and his nostrils flared like an eager bull's.

"You may think you serve Our Lord, but you have been misled," Father Gerard said.

I could see that there was actual compassion in the holy man's eyes. Father Gerard truly believed that these men had been misled. From his chair, he looked as though he was preaching to a wayward flock, trying with all his might to lead them toward the right path.

"Witches are employed by the devil to turn the hearts of men to evil," said Father Gerard. "Just as Cain slew Abel for the lust of a witch. That single act led him to commit the first murder. Witches have been the devil's chief weapon against the saving grace of God and entry into the Kingdom of Heaven."

In the Bible, as well as the Quran and a few other works, the story goes that Cain and Abel were the sons of Adam and Eve. Cain, the elder, tilled the soil. Abel, the younger, was a shepherd. The stories go on to say that after God chose Abel's sacrifice over Cain's, Cain slew his brother. The Bible doesn't explain why or what the sacrifice was for. Some believed that it was over a woman both brothers wanted to marry, and that the sacrifice each presented was for the honor of her hand. If this story was true, and I had no way of knowing, then the first murder was a crime of passion. This was also the first time I'd ever heard someone postulate that the woman was a witch.

"The demon spawn must be eradicated from the world," continued Father Gerard. "And when my brothers find the Holy Grail, they will be."

The nerve in Arthur's corded neck worked as he glared down at the cross on the man's chest. "Geraint? Percival? Will you show this man some medieval hospitality?"

Geraint came forward without any hesitation. Percival sighed, but he did as his leader bade. They lifted Father Gerard up by his armpits and led him out of the room.

Arthur took a breath. Then he motioned me over to the Round Table. I still held the scroll in my hand. He swept his hand toward it, indicating I should get to the job he'd brought me in for. But I held my ground.

"What are you going to do to him? Torture him?"

"Yes." Arthur breathed the word.

I reared back, my body turning toward the door the knights and the priest had exited.

"We're at war, Nia. The opposition is killing innocent witches, men, and children. I will forfeit one life if it will protect hundreds."

I hated his reasoning. It was the reasoning of so many leaders who came before him. I had saved Father Gerard's life just a day ago. But it seemed he'd been taking innocent lives before that, and would continue to do so if he were let outside of these castle walls.

I had no remorse for the nameless, faceless Templars who lay dying on the ground back in that cave. But neither did they have a care for the countless bones stacked in the corners and in the fire pit. Nor the tens of thousands of human lives forfeited because a group of fearful religious, political, or tribal leaders had tried to validate their existential angst by culling the herd after they realized their worldview was mistaken and they weren't in control after all.

I closed my eyes. I didn't believe in prayer, but I

took a moment of silence to settle my conscience. Then I walked to the table and got to work.

I laid the scroll down on the table. Miraculously, it had been untouched by the waters. I carefully unfurled the document, and the symbols jumped out at me.

"What does it say?" Arthur asked.

"I'm not Google Translate. Just give me a second."

For most, cuneiform was the oldest form of writing. I knew symbols from before that time. These weren't those symbols. The vast amount of curves and lines that were collected in my head often made me pause a moment to orient myself to which dialect I was looking at.

I had been rushed in the temple and had only given the scroll a cursory look before our lives had been placed in peril. A closer look at the body of the text told me I wouldn't need to reach back too far in my memory to translate this. Nor would I need a software app to discern the words.

I looked up from the scroll at the warriors before me. "This is French."

Arthur frowned. Then he came and peered over my shoulder. "Oh."

"Oh? That's all you have to say is *Oh?*" I glared at

him. Then I cocked my head to the side and studied him. "Wait, why are you saying *Oh?* Why aren't you surprised?"

Arthur rubbed the golden whiskers on his chin. But he didn't answer.

"Wait a minute," I said, taking a step from the table and thinking back in time. "The Knights Templar was formed in France. Why would you think they would've written anything in an ancient script?"

Lance and Gawain sat watchful in the corner as Gwin and Morgan healed them. Young Tristan sat in a seat alongside his father and the elderly Bedivere and Kay. They all held tight lips. No one met my gaze.

"What aren't you all telling me?"

"Would you read the message please?" Arthur demanded.

"Why can't you? Like I said, it's French."

When they were young and their fathers still held the titled seats, the young knights were allowed to further their education and experience of the world. Most didn't, preferring to stay close to home and their duties. But I knew Arthur had gone to Cambridge for a couple of years in the late nineteenth century. Even before that, he'd had a world-class education taught by those who'd lived it. He'd had two hundred years to learn an easy Romance language like French.

"It's in Old French," Arthur said.

I looked down at the scroll. It was indeed an older version of modern French. The handwriting was likely a man's with large blocky letters. It was in the form of a letter with a salutation at the top and a scrawled signature at the bottom. This language was spoken from the eighth to the fourteenth centuries.

"This script looks like it's from the late ninth century," I said.

Arthur's face was no longer blank. He looked at me like he often did Morgan. As though he were at the edge of his patience and life would be easier if he simply strangled me. "Read it."

"But don't you get it? The Knights Templar weren't formed until the eleventh century," I said. "It can't be written by any of them."

Again, I got crickets. But instead of getting mad, I was intrigued. History told that the Knights Templar had been formed by Hugues de Payens, a nobleman from Champagne, France, sometime around the early eleventh century. The Templars' mission had been to protect pilgrims on their journeys to and from the holy land of Jerusalem, specifically to

Temple Mount or Solomon's Temple. In fact, it was how they got their names. The Poor Knights of the Temple of King Solomon.

I decided that if no one was going to help me in unraveling the mystery, I might as well skip to the end. And when I did, things got curiouser and curiouser.

"It's signed by a man named…" I squinted. "Joseph de Paganis. Wow, that's remarkably close to Hugues de Payens. Could this be a relative?"

I'd lost count of how many times I'd looked up from my place at the teacher's lectern to find a class full of students who already knew the lecture at hand.

"Okay, I'm not reading another word unless you give me something in return."

Sir Kay looked to Arthur, who then nodded.

"The Knights Templar were not founded by Hugues de Payens," said the older knight. "They are a much older organization. Once upon a time, very long ago, their mission was pure. They protected pilgrims as they journeyed."

"Before the Crusades, you mean?" I asked.

Sir Kay nodded.

"So who were *those* knights protecting pilgrims from?"

"The people weren't pilgrims," Arthur said. "They were witches. There have always been witches in this world. Alongside them were the men who took up arms to protect them from those who saw them as evil."

I had only known witches and wizards on the grounds of Camelot. I had never met one on the outside, though I knew they had been there. A witch or wizard off a ley line for too long was vulnerable, just like two Immortals who stayed together. If they had to move over great distances and couldn't jump the wormhole of a ley line, it made sense that they'd need muscle as protection.

"The mission of the knights predates the original Arthur, as does magic," said Sir Kay. "There have always been brave men risking their lives to protect the magical kind. With the rise of the Roman Catholic Church, there also came the rise of men of opportunity. Those men don't like the competition for their beliefs. Joseph de Paganis was indeed Hugues de Payens."

Mind. Blown. I'd stepped on the neck bone of a historical legend back in those caves. It was his suicide note that I held in my hands. Oh, what a museum wouldn't give for this document. But Sir

Kay wasn't finished with his tale or his mental bomb droppings.

"He was a descendant of a witch."

"And he was a traitor to his people," Arthur said. "He joined with the Church and began searching out anything and anyone magical and erasing them from the world."

"Why?" I asked.

"Same reason men fight over imaginary lines drawn in the sand," said Arthur. "For power and dominion over each other. Now"—Arthur took another deep breath as though he were reaching out once more for patience—"will you read the scroll please?"

I looked again at the scroll. Now that I knew the language I was working with, the words began to fit themselves together and take shape.

"It begins 'Dear Father, Forgive me for my sins. I have betrayed you, my father, my sister, and the Holy One. The serpent stole my heart and blinded my eyes. But even in my darkest hours I did not betray the Grail. It remains safe at home. I only hope that when I meet you in the Holy Kingdom, you can accept me back into your graces. Your son, Joseph de Paganis.'"

"At home?" Sir Kay asked. "Which home?"

"We searched Glastonbury," Arthur said. "If the Grail were there, we would've found it."

"What about Champagne?" offered Sir Bedivere.

Arthur shook his head. "Lady Merida still resides there. We were in contact with her just days ago."

"She is his descendant," said Bedivere. "She may be keeping details from us. Her loyalty lies with her maternal ancestor. It's worth a physical visit. To see if you can find anything."

Arthur thought for a moment. "Rest up. We'll leave at first light." Then he turned to me as though he'd forgotten I was there. "I don't suppose we can part ways now and you won't interfere?"

"You're a really smart man," I said. "And you know I'm a smart woman, even though you're only giving me partial clues. I know that champagne is not only a delicious beverage, it's also a province in France. And it also happens to be the birthplace of Hugues de Payens."

"What do you want, Nia?"

"What every educated, self-aware, self-sufficient woman wants—a little adventure. I'm coming along."

He took another breath. "Fine. We may still need your translation skills."

Worked for me.

Arthur turned away from me and began planning with the other knights. Loren came up beside me.

"Champagne, France?" she asked.

"Yep."

"You sure you can handle France?"

"Why wouldn't I be able to handle France?"

"You know..." She shrugged. "A certain Fine-Ass Frenchie who asked for space."

"I can go to France. He can't have a whole country to himself."

Loren held up her hands. "Okay then."

I crossed my arms over my chest. "Okay then."

CHAPTER FIFTEEN

When I came down to the throne room the next morning, Loren was standing just outside the door looking at a portrait of a blond-haired knight. The placard in gold at the bottom read Sir Galahad, first of his name. Across his heart, he held a sword.

Loren looked down at the tip of her father's cane where her great-grandfather's sword protruded. "I thought my mother left me with nothing but her hair color, eyes, and those bedtime stories. But in truth, she left me with a magical sword."

She held the sword up in the morning light. It twinkled.

"Remember that part in the Arthur stories where

the Lady in the Lake gives King Arthur Excalibur?" Loren said.

"You mean the sword in the stone?" I asked.

"No. He originally got it from her in the lake."

I didn't know the Arthurian stories that well. When I knew that a story was based on the truth, I tended to go to the source instead of the fictional reference. I knew that the Knights of the Round Table all had swords that were imbued with magic. The magic in the swords would only respond to the knight it chose to handle it. For years, Loren had been wielding a magical sword and hadn't known it.

"When Arthur pulled the sword, he became king." Her blue gaze met mine. "Since the Lady in the Lake gave it to me last night, do you think that makes me a queen?"

I snorted.

"At least a princess?"

"This isn't a kingdom anymore," I said.

"Maybe a knight, then? Sir Loren. I like the sound of that."

"Women can't be knights," Morgan said, coming up to stand beside us. "In the past, witches fought alongside the knights, like my grandmother Morgana. And even Arthur's grandmother Mara. She was a great witch and fought off the Roman invaders. But after the Scottish North Berwick Witch Trials, the Arthurs felt it was better to keep us under lock and key than to allow us precious flowers to fight beside them in battle."

Morgan glared at the portraits of Arthur the Second, and beside it, his son Arthur the Third. Said Arthur approached alongside Geraint and Percival. Arthur eyed Morgan warily. But this morning, Morgan didn't protest or press her cause. She rolled her eyes and headed down the hall as Gwin came down the staircase.

"Be safe," Morgan said as she embraced her sister.

"There will be no danger," said Gwin. "Very few even know about the chateau."

We were headed to Champagne, France. To the estate of Hugues de Payens, whom history believed started the Knights Templar, but who I'd just learned was truly named Joseph de Paganis. The estate was on a ley line. A witch of Gwin's power could open a door and let us travel across the line that stretched from the castle to the chateau.

Tension ran off Arthur's shoulders as he eyed Gwin. I knew he wished there were a man who had this door-opening ability so he didn't have to put a woman at risk.

"Once we go through, you'll stay by my side," Arthur said to Gwin.

"Of course, my lord."

"There should be no danger, but I won't put your life at risk."

"I'll do as you say." She nodded, her expression docile and obedient.

Arthur looked down. His forehead wrinkled. His hand fidgeted with the hilt of his sword. "When we get back, there's something I'd like to discuss with you about the future."

Gwin nodded. Her countenance was businesslike, as was Arthur's. "Yes, my lord." And then her face froze.

Over Arthur's shoulder stood Lance. Lance and Gwin's gazes caught and held. Lance looked at the closeness of his leader and the woman he was so clearly interested in. He clenched his jaw, but he didn't say anything.

"You should be resting," Arthur said, turning to his second. "You're not your best self yet."

Lance's chin shot up in defiance. "I'm healed, and I can take my place. You need the manpower."

Arthur looked about to argue, but then decided against it.

"This is so much better than my mother's

bedtime stories," Loren whispered as we both stood by watching the drama unfold.

We followed the three as they walked in a stiff triangle into the throne room. Geraint waited at a door on the far side of the room. Just stepping near the door made the hairs on the back of my neck stand up.

"It's the energy of the ley line," Gwin said. "We are all energy beings beneath our skin. This is the stuff that our souls are made of. We all interact with it differently."

She turned to Loren.

"You may be disoriented on the other side," Gwin said. "It hits those with more human blood harder since they are the most diluted. I don't mean that in an offensive way."

"None taken," said Loren.

"What about me?" I asked.

"What about you?" Gwin asked.

I opened my mouth to tell her that I didn't have a soul, but the words wouldn't come through my lips. They didn't feel right. Plus, I'd had no trouble traveling by ley line the other night. Maybe Aleph, the oldest Immortal, was wrong. She believed we didn't have souls because we were not humans. She believed we came from angels.

Igraine came into the room holding a piece of dark material in her hand. She handed it to Gwin. "I almost forgot. You'll need this."

The shawl was made of fine lace, woven intricately. The color was black as a shadow. It was a widow's shawl. "What's this for?" Gwin frowned.

"To give your condolences, of course. Lady Merida is with your husband now."

We all stared at Igraine. Her gaze was clouded over. She was in a trance. She was seeing a vision.

Gwin looked to Arthur, who drew his sword. A chorus of metal becoming unsheathed sounded all around us. The men stepped forward and opened the door. It was black inside, but the wind howled, trying to suck me in. Gwin closed her eyes and began a chant.

The energy in the room increased. It was like drinking the strongest shot of espresso in my life. Make that a double.

One by one, we went in. First Arthur and Gwin. I was caught up in the middle, after Lance and between Loren and Geraint. Stepping into the darkness, I felt like I'd been sleeping my whole life. The moment the energy sparked my blood was when I woke up.

Inside the darkness, I was blinded by a light. It

was bright, but it didn't hurt my eyes. It was soft. When I took another step, it was gone, and I felt an aching sense of loneliness.

"You okay?" I asked Loren once I caught my breath.

She stared at me in a daze. Then she blinked. Her body shuddered like a current went through it. I reached out to touch her, and energy zapped my fingers like I'd stuck my hand into a socket.

"Ow." I jerked my hand away from her.

We both stared at my red fingertip. Loren's eyes were bright like she'd taken a hit of some good drugs. She turned back to the door, but the light had returned to darkness. The energy had died. Geraint closed the door and ushered us on.

We were in a small chapel, but the room looked as though it had gone through a hurricane.

"Templars," Arthur growled.

"How could they know to come to this place?" asked Geraint. "History records that de Payens was on their side. They shouldn't have thought to look for the Grail here."

"Regardless of whether he repented or not," Arthur said, "he was a traitor to his kind. We need to find Lady Merida."

"Who's Lady Merida?" Loren asked.

As if she heard her name spoken, a woman moaned. The knights rushed toward the sound.

An elderly woman was sprawled out on the floor, left discarded like a doll after a child's rough play. Arthur hurried to her, kneeling and cradling her weak frame in his arms.

"Gwin," Arthur called. "We need your help."

But Gwin stood frozen in place, looking down at the woman.

"Gwin," snapped Arthur.

But she didn't budge. She stared down at the woman, her lips trembling, her eyes watering.

Lance approached her, taking her face in his hand. "Gwin," he said gently. "She needs you."

"I can't," sobbed Gwin.

"Of course you can," Lance said. "You're the bravest woman I know, the strongest, too. Your magic will heal her. It will save her life."

But Gwin shook her head, the tears falling in earnest now.

"Gwin, she'll die if you don't—"

"You don't understand," Gwin said. "My magic can't help her. I can only heal those who have magic."

"She's a witch," Lance said, sounding confused. "Magic flows through her veins."

Gwin shook her head. "Her powers are gone."

"That's not possible," Arthur said.

"Dark magic," whispered Geraint. His voice was tinged with horror.

"Dark magic?" I asked.

It wasn't a word I'd heard often, not since the rule of the first Arthur. Witches and wizards abided by a code. They healed, they helped, and they made things better. In essence, it was much like the Hippocratic Oath of do no harm. That was, of course, unless harm was heading their way. Dark magic was dangerous, abusive, deadly. It was only used to hurt, to weaken, and to kill.

"But who?" Arthur said.

It was then Lady Merida whispered a single word. A word that took all the air out of the room. After a moment, she said it again. It was the last word she spoke as she took her final breath.

"Merlin."

CHAPTER SIXTEEN

The rain came down in light pats as the fire outside the chateau blazed. I watched from the window as Geraint stoked the flames, keeping them burning bright as the fire consumed Lady Merida's body.

"He would've died if I hadn't done it," Gwin said.

"But it's dark magic," Arthur said.

Gwin shook her head. "I don't believe magic has a light or dark side. That comes from the user."

"He's the one who's dark," growled Lance. "You should not have allowed him to violate you in such a way."

The fire outside flared brighter behind Lance as though to punctuate his statement. As Gwin had said before we'd walked into a door and across a ley line, magic was the energy within us. That energy could transport a body across space and time. It could be imbued into objects directly by witches, or through the perpetual worship of ordinary human beings. And, apparently, it could be siphoned from one person into another.

Merlin had siphoned what was left of the elder witch's magic and left her to die. It fit the pattern that he had probably done this with the dead witch Gwin and Arthur had found days earlier. And most likely the other unsolved cases of missing elder and off-grid witches for the last two decades. It was a tactic he'd learned from Gwin. But she had used it for good. She had given him some of her magic when he was ill to keep him alive.

"He didn't violate me," Gwin protested, but her certainty sounded strangled as the words came from her throat. "He would've died if I hadn't done it. I did what I had to do to protect our people and their heir."

I turned to Arthur. Her words sounded so much like his. Arthur, who had last night sent a man into the dungeons to be tortured until he gave up information. He'd done it to protect his people, he'd said. Arthur grit his teeth as he took in the situation before him.

"That parasitic bastard still has you brainwashed," said Lance, not caring he was calling out his leader's flesh and blood. "Even after all these years."

Fire flashed in Gwin's eyes. "I have my own mind. Just because it doesn't tell me to do what you want doesn't mean I can't think for myself."

I had never seen this side of Gwin. Apparently, Lance had, because he stepped up to her, toe to toe.

"He took advantage of your good heart. You could never see when someone was trying to manipulate you."

"At least he cared enough to try," Gwin shot back.

Lance turned his face aside as though she'd slapped him.

"That's enough, you two," Arthur said, coming between them.

Lance paced to the other side of the room away from us all. Gwin watched him go. The fire in her eyes died and turned to a remorseful longing as she watched him retreat.

"You told me he was still alive," Arthur said to her. "This is how you knew?"

Gwin nodded. "I suspected, but I didn't know for sure. I could feel the link with him since he shares some of my spirit. It had grown weaker and weaker over the years, but I still felt something of him."

In the corner, Lance made a noise that sounded like he was choking.

"You should've come to me, Gwin," Arthur said.

"I did," she protested.

"No." Arthur shook his head. "Before this. After he asked for your very soul."

"In sickness and health, for better or worse—it's all part of the marriage contract." Gwin looked down at her hands. "You've said many times that a good knight always puts the good of the kingdom before himself."

"You're not a knight."

Gwin looked up at him with a wry smile that reminded me of her sister. "Yes, I am. Just because I don't carry a sword and run off into battle doesn't mean I'm not. Just like you said to Morgan the other night—we're at war, and we must tend to those who have fallen, not leave them behind."

Arthur shook his head and pointed out the window at the raging fire. "This was wrong, Gwin. He's siphoning off their power and taking it for himself."

"Like some kind of vampire," muttered Lance.

"I'm sure he did it to survive," Gwin said.

"Tell that to Lady Merida," Lance said hotly. "Tell that to Lady Circe. Tell that to the family we found months ago who was murdered. We thought it was the Templars, but there was something off about it. I should've smelled that weasel—"

"Enough," Arthur said.

"He did this," Lance said, advancing toward his leader. "He's after the Grail. And if he gets his hands on it and its power..."

Arthur ran his hands over his face. "We'll find the Grail before he does. Sir Joseph must've left a clue, *something*, here."

"What might a clue look like?" Loren asked. She was standing off in a corner looking up. "Maybe something out of place? Maybe something from Arthurian Legends in a French chateau?"

We all turned our attention in the direction of her gaze. Up on the wall was a crest. Embedded in the crest were the images of a sword, a shield, a cross, and a lamb.

"I recognize that from when I was younger," Loren said. "My mother had a picture of it."

"It's the crest of Glastonbury."

Arthur stormed over and, with one mighty pounding, busted the wall down. But the moment the plaster crumbled, he jerked his hand back as though there were fire inside.

Lance and Gwin took a step back as well. Even Loren took a step to the side, rubbing her head as though she were coming down with a migraine.

I stepped up to the hole in the wall. Inside was a jar. But surrounding the jar was a fist-sized pale blue rock. A bluestone.

If this was the house of a witch, what was that kryptonite doing in the walls? Whatever was in that jar was something that someone didn't want another with witch's blood to see. I reached in and pulled out the jar.

We all retreated to the far side of the room. I set the jar on the table and reached into my bag for my gloves. Arthur sighed, his jaw tense as he waited, knowing I wouldn't touch the ancient document inside the jar without protection.

Once I was gloved up, I carefully unfolded the ancient document on a table. The symbols jumped out at me, calling upon various parts of my brain. They didn't seem to adhere to any one language, but I did catch a name.

"It says it was written by a Joseph...Joseph of..."

"Glastonbury?" asked Lance. "There was a knight by the name of Joseph of Glastonbury."

"Not Glastonbury," I said. "Arimathea."

"It's the same man," Arthur said.

"Joseph of Arimathea?" I said. "From the Bible? The man who buried Jesus?"

Surprisingly, I remembered the man. His name was actually Joseph of Marmorica. He was an Egyptian merchant and a relative of Jesus on his mother's side. Everyone during that time knew Joseph. He was a wealthy man and on the council of Sanhedrin. The same council that voted for Jesus to be put to death. Joseph had been working on the inside of the council to get his nephew leniency. As we all know, that didn't work, and Jesus was crucified.

History forgot about Joseph. So did I. But the knights didn't seem too surprised to hear his name mentioned.

"Are you saying Joseph of Arimathea came here?" I asked Arthur, but it was Gwin who answered.

"This was his home," Gwin said. "He lived here with his wife and family."

She looked like she wanted to say more, but she quieted with a look from Arthur.

"And he was in Glastonbury before that?" I asked.

"Many times," Lance said. "Once with his nephew, a young man named Yeshua, who became known to the world as Jesus Christ, our Lord and Savior."

"There's not much mention of the life of Christ between his birth and when he began preaching the gospel," Arthur said. "But he worked with his father and did some traveling with his merchant uncle during those times. Sometime after the crucifixion, Joseph came to settle here with his family."

"That's not possible. Jesus died in 36 A.D. This was written around 300 A.D.

Arthur nodded. "Joseph of Arimathea had witch's blood in his veins."

"Wait, wait, wait. Hold up," I said. "Are you saying that Jesus had witch's blood?"

Arthur didn't answer that question. He posed another. "What does the scroll say?"

I turned my attention back to it. Now that I had a reference that the author could indeed be writing in a hodgepodge of three different languages, like an ancient form of Spanglish, the words came somewhat easier. Some looked Aramaic and then there was also a bit of Egyptian mixed in with...was that Celtic?

But the patterns of the languages did not follow

the rules. At some points, the Aramaic looked old, as though it could be Galilean. And the Egyptian wasn't the Coptic that had fused with the Greek alphabet. But it was all written by the same hand. It was as though whoever wrote this had lived a very long life in many different places. And then I realized something truly horrible.

"It's a poem." I groaned.

Which was just great. Next to riddles, poems were my least favorite form of literacy. I concentrated on the first stanza. I already had the first line translated as it was the author giving a shout-out and telling everyone his name. But the next lines had me tripped up grammatically.

"The which had grace...which saved in the...city of...Sarras... the spiritual place."

But "which" was spelled two separate ways. I had to assume that one of these translations was a noun and the other a preposition. I began again.

"This is Joseph of Arimathea. The witch had grace which was saved in the City of Sarras in the spiritual place."

"Keep going," Arthur said.

I focused on the second stanza. "They were afraid to the form of one dead three hundred years. But I said..."

I stared. The verb and subject agreement was horrible in this poem.

"But Joseph said, 'A man like you, look on me and have no fear," Loren finished for me.

We all turned to her.

"I know this poem," she said. "The City of Sarras. It's one of the obscure romance poems about the Knights of the Round Table. My mother used to read them to me when I was a little girl. It was in a book."

"This scroll was in a book?" I said.

"Yes, but you skipped the beginning where it talks about Galahad, Bors, and Percival going to the Castle Carbonek to eat with King Pelles."

I looked at the scroll. "That's not here? What comes next in your version? After the part about having no fear?"

"Um..." Loren scrunched her nose and looked up, as though she was reciting the poem from the beginning. "'Then they saw two angels standing there, wax candles in their hair?' Or maybe it was in their hand? 'And Joseph of Arimathea between that twain did stand.'"

I followed along with her. It was a near perfect translation.

The next part Loren recited about knights coming to the table to eat was not in the scroll.

There was a hodgepodge of the next parts where Loren remembered more of the knights drinking from the Grail. But the scroll told a different tale.

"Too sweet for earth, my savior was. Too marvelous to behold. But after Night, the day and here in the realm of Logres the Grail cannot stay."

"So it *was* here," said Arthur. "But Joseph moved it? Does it say where?"

I read on. "Til to Sarras you sail the sea. Til you come where you and I stood face-to-face. Til you stand in the City of Sarras in the Spiritual Place."

"So the Grail is in Sarras?" Lance asked.

"Where's Sarras?" Gwin said.

"I don't know," Arthur said.

"Pull up Google Maps." Loren snapped her fingers.

I hung back, waiting patiently. Knowing with certainty they wouldn't find the ancient city of Sarras on any map.

Arthur's gaze found mine. He quirked his brow in question.

"Yeah, I know where it is," I said. "And I call shotgun."

CHAPTER SEVENTEEN

The moment we stepped through the door from Champagne and back into the throne room of Camelot, we all parted ways. Gwin and Lance went in opposite directions from each other, neither saying a word.

Arthur called the remaining knights to him. They took their seats around the table and were informed of Merlin being alive, as well as of his treachery. Arthur didn't speak harshly of Gwin's role in the events, playing her up as a victim instead of an accomplice.

I knew that the brothers hadn't always seen eye to eye. I'd had the same impression of the elder prince of Camelot that Lance had—that he was a bit entitled. But I had always chalked that up to his poor health and fragility. Just look at the mountain of a father and younger brother he had to measure up to.

The shock of Merlin's treachery was not taken lightly by the knights. They hadn't dealt with dark magic in hundreds of years. Now they had to contend with a vampiric wizard, whose end they did not know, as well as the ever-advancing Templar army, who wanted to wipe their kind off the face of the earth. It was a lot to deal with.

I hung back with Loren but felt a buzzing in my pocket. I looked down at my cell phone. My thumb hovered over the *talk* key.

"If you don't press that button, so help me, I will reach down your throat and pull out your spirit and do it myself."

I rolled my eyes at Loren. But then I went out into the hallway and pressed the button. I didn't mull over my salutation approach this time. I kept it simple.

"Hey," I said.

"I've been thinking about you all week," Tres said.

"And yet you're only calling now?"

"You were at sea."

"I called yesterday, or did you not get the message from your guard dog?"

Tres chuckled. As he did, a bit of static mixed into the reception. I held my breath and went still. Cell communication was notoriously iffy when it came between two Immortals. But when he spoke again, his voice was crystal clear.

"My guard dog, as you call her, keeps away the unwanted attention I receive on an hourly basis. The moment she handed me your note, I called you. Because I want your attention on a moment-to-moment basis."

"You do?" My voice came out breathy, like one of the damsels of the medieval romances Loren loved as a child.

"Where are you? I'll hop on my yacht, or my jet, and come to you."

"You can't," I said.

"Why? Are you in some tomb in a native land?"

"Pretty much." I looked around at the ancient sconces on the walls. "I'm in Camelot with the knights."

Silence. I wondered if we'd lost the connection, so I stared at the bars on the phone. They were all present and high. And then...

"Is this going to have to be a rescue mission? Are you in the dungeon?"

"No." I laughed, pressing the phone to my ear. "I

was invited. The Arthur needed a favor that only my specialized skills could manage."

"Specialized skills?"

"Translations. He needed a couple of scrolls translated, and I do specialize in ancient tongues."

"Hmm. I'd like to teach you my ancient tongue. When will you be leaving there?"

"I'm actually leaving in the morning, but we're going on a quest."

"He invited you to the castle and on one of his quests? Are you sure he's not trying to get you killed?"

"Be kinda hard to do, my being Immortal and all."

I thought back to Igraine's words and her vision. That only seven Immortals would return to the garden. She'd been right about Merida now being with Merlin, though in a completely unexpected way. That was the thing about visions of the future and past. They weren't always clear.

I wondered if I should tell Tres about what I'd learned? Or maybe about the dream I'd had of us all in a garden. A dream where he and Zane looked like they were the best of friends? Probably not.

"Where are you headed off to?" Tres asked. "I

have some time off. Maybe I can tag along? Or meet you once your mission is complete?"

"We're headed to Iraq."

"You're going into a war zone?"

The city of Sarras was in what was once known as the Kingdom of Babylon, better known today as Iraq. But we weren't just headed to see the palaces in Baghdad, or the waterfalls of Erbil, or the shrines of Karbala. The current name of Sarras was Mosul, an ISIS stronghold. The site of the military operation led by the United States and Coalition Forces to dislodge and defeat the Islamic State.

"You are not making dating you easy, Dr. Rivers."

Tres and I had been at each other's throats for hundreds of years. We were natural enemies. He was a land developer intent on progress. I was a conservationist out to protect every bit of history from being erased.

But before that, we'd been lovers. We may have even been in love? I couldn't remember.

He could remember the details. But he'd decided to keep our past in the past and start anew. So, we were dating. Kinda.

"If I didn't know any better," he said, "I'd think you were trying to keep me at arm's length."

"I'm not."

I wasn't. It was just that something always came between us as we tried to move closer to each other. True, that something was usually put in place by me.

"I'd like to see you again," I said. "But maybe not with a horde of martial artists trying to mix our bones in a stew or gods raising the dead. You know, something normal."

"I think we left normal a couple of centuries ago."

I had no idea what a normal relationship looked like. Dinner and a movie where we watched a historical adaptation and pointed out all the flaws we knew were wrong because we'd seen them with our own eyes? Maybe a walk along a beach hand in hand where we could recount how we'd witnessed the skyline change over the centuries. Or maybe we could just stay in and talk about our shared past.

In any case, I wanted that. I wanted a little normal in my life. A moment to slow down and be a woman with a man who wasn't lying to me or trying to get something from me.

"I'll plan something," he said.

"I look forward to it."

We got off the line, and I held the warm phone in my palm for a moment. There was a bubbling in my chest and a lightness in my head. Most might call it anticipation. I balled my fists together and pressed them into my chest.

When I looked around, Loren was nowhere to be found. But there was another figure lurking in the shadows.

"Hey," I said. "How're you holding up?"

Lance had his eyes locked on a picture of Merlin and Gwin together. Unlike Arthur, Merlin had dark hair crowning his head and no facial hair at his chin. His head looked too big for his body, as though his frame had been made for a warrior but it never quite filled out. The portrait looked like it could be their wedding photo. Merlin had the entitled tilt to his chin. Gwin had the stoic lift to her mouth. Neither of them smiled.

"You know I've loved that woman since the first time I laid eyes on her," Lance said.

"Does she know that?" I asked him.

"She was always so preoccupied saving anyone who was sick or wounded. Merlin took up most of her time. I never needed her like that. Not her magic or her healing. I just wanted her heart."

"Tell her that," I said. "Exactly like you just said to me."

Lance turned to look at me as though he were seeing me for the first time since he began talking.

"Why? She'll go back to him. Even after all he's done. She'll rationalize his actions. And she'll stand by his side, because he needs her. He's used her all her life, and now I see to what extent. I'm going to kill the bastard. Even if she hates me for it. At least then she'll be free of him."

He pushed off the wall and headed down the hall. Intention was in his every step. His fists were balled at his side with what looked like anticipation.

CHAPTER EIGHTEEN

Rain pitter-pattered on the castle window the next morning. My sleep had been dreamless since coming from Greece. Tres had yet to show up in a dream. He preferred to find me in reality. Zane hadn't been back in my dreams since he'd found me in Athens kissing someone else's lips.

Before that, I'd dreamed nearly every night of my ex. Not sex dreams—well, most of them weren't. Mainly memories of our time together.

Just the little things. Like the time we'd gone diving in the Coral Reef. I'd spent the day taking samples of plant life while he'd mixed primaries to capture the seascape. I dreamed of the times we'd walked hand in hand on beaches; the white sand of

Oahu, the pink sands of the southern Philippines, and the black sands of Vik in Iceland. I dreamed of us lying on our backs looking up at the Aurora Borealis.

Yeah, the little things.

Zane was an incurable romantic. Even though we'd had to spend most of our time apart due to the allergy, he'd made sure I'd always felt his presence with gifts, letters, and, later, text messages. There were always plans on the horizon. He'd always have a part of my soul. But I couldn't feel his presence now.

Which was understandable. We weren't together anymore. Not as lovers, anyway. But he'd always been my friend, even during the in between times when we weren't together. He was the only family I had.

I lay in this strange bed alone. I spent much of my life in single-occupancy hotel rooms. Spread out alone in a two-man tent on a dig. But for the first time in a long time, in this castle filled with people, I felt alone.

I heard the bustle of the castle above me. A deep male voice barking out unintelligible orders. The delighted squeal of a child. The trilling laugh of a woman, accompanied by the low growl of a man.

The sounds of life drifted down through the walls. I could make out the individual tones of different people laughing in a chorus. Their voices came together like practiced instruments playing a familiar tune. I scrubbed my hand over my face and pushed myself out of the bed.

After getting dressed and strapping on a dagger to each hip, placing a blade in each boot, and then strapping my sais over my shoulders, I made my way up to the throne room. We were headed into a war zone today, and I wanted to be prepared.

Outside the throne room, I saw a cluster of women. I immediately recognized the white hair of Igraine as she tilted her head to the side in concern. Standing beside her was the dark-haired Morgan. Her jaw was clenched as though she was trying to hold her tongue. Between them were two golden-haired beauties—Gwin and Loren.

Gwin's light eyes looked defeated, but her lips were pressed in a resolute line. Beside her, Loren rubbed her back in a move of solidarity. They looked like a tight-knit unit as they stood outside the knights' stronghold. They looked like a family of women who had each other's backs, quite literally.

I chewed at the inside of my lip as I watched Loren speak to Gwin. When Loren finished speaking, her eyes twinkled like they did when she'd said something particularly clever. Igraine's ample bosom trembled with a light laugh. Morgan quirked an eyebrow, a reluctant grin tugging at the corner of her mouth. Gwin's thin lips loosened just a bit in what I thought might be an attempt at a smile.

I stood across the room, unsure of whether to go into the room full of knights or to cross the divide and join my best friend. But then Loren stepped in front of Igraine, effectively closing the circle and closing me out.

I smoothed my hand over the blades at my sides, seeking their cold comfort. Turning myself toward the mission, I picked up my feet to make my way into the throne room.

"Hey," Loren called.

I looked up as she broke away from the group, her true family. As she walked away from Gwin and Morgan in the background, I saw the family resemblance even more prominently. Their eyes were shaped the same. The descendants of Galahad all had a haughty air to their chins, even though they carried themselves differently. Morgan was full of defiance, Gwin full of compassion, and Loren filled with mischief.

Loren came to stand before me, that mischievous

grin spread across her face. But the moment it reached up to her eyes, it fell. "What's wrong?"

"What do you mean?" I asked.

"You've got the look," she said.

"What look?"

"The same look you had after we left Greece." She frowned. "Did you call Zane?"

"No." My tone may have been a bit defensive. Loren had said she thought Zane and I were codependent. We obviously weren't if I was here alone and he was off somewhere… doing whatever he was doing without me. I decided to turn the tables on her. "Where'd you spend your night? Or better yet, with whom?"

I wondered if I needed to check in on Gawain. Knights healed fast, too, thanks to the magic in their veins as well as the reinforcements that a witch could give to them.

"I had a sleepover with the kids," Loren said. "It was awesome. We slept in the armory and built forts."

"The armory?"

"It's the safest place in the castle." She shrugged.

"It seems like you're really fitting in here."

Again, she shrugged. "There's something that feels familiar about this place."

"I was thinking maybe you should stay behind today. There's more questions you want to have answered about your mother. This isn't so much a magical mission as it is entering a militarized zone."

"Why are we having this conversation again?" Loren asked. "If I were going into a militarized zone, would you be behind me?"

"That's different."

"Because you're Immortal? Well, it turns out I'm not human anymore. I've got some magic in me, too."

"Loren." I sighed.

"This is the third time you've tried to get rid of me. Is it because of the mascara stain on your Saint Laurent blouse?"

"No. Wait! What?"

"Is it that you think I'm competition for Tres? Because I swear—my breasts, they just perk up at the sign of millions. I can't help it."

She took in a breath and her chest rose. Then she tried to slump her arsenal in to no avail. A giggle escaped my lips as I watched her antics. Then I chuckled. Next came a full-blown laugh. I reached out and wrapped her in my arms.

"I know you worry about me," Loren said into my shoulder. "If I stayed behind, you'd worry what I might get into. If you went without me, I'd worry about you. Isn't it better if we just stick together?"

I sighed again as I let her go.

"Look, I'll be smart," she said. "I won't do anything unnecessarily heroic, which will be a challenge for me because we all know how awesome I am. Plus, I promised Morgan I'd represent the Galahad Girls. It rankles Arthur to have women infiltrate his little boy band."

Speaking of the king, he came to the doorway. His eyes glanced over Loren and me with barely checked disdain. Then went to the corner where Gwin stood.

"We're ready," he said, his voice thick.

It was obvious he didn't want any of us on this mission. But his hands were tied. He needed Gwin to open the doorway. He needed me to be his tour guide. And I wasn't going anywhere without Loren.

So the three of us took a step forward. Loren and I practically skipped into the room. Gwin took a wobbly step forward. But by the second step, her legs were sure.

Morgan took a step behind her, but one look from Arthur and the dark-haired beauty stutter-stepped and stopped. That defiant chin looked as though it would cut granite.

"You're not coming with us," Arthur said. "And that's final."

"Two witches against one is far better odds," Morgan said.

"I'd prefer it was no witches, but we need Gwin to open the ley line. And she still has a connection to Merlin. She'll be able to tell us if he's near."

"But doesn't that mean he'll know where she is?" Morgan asked. "Basically making her bait."

"As I said, it's unavoidable. And she'll have the full contingent of the knights to protect her. She'll also stay on the holy ground of the temple connected to the ley line and evacuate at the first sign of danger. We'll find our own way back in that case."

This he spoke directly to Gwin. She took a deep breath and nodded once.

Morgan opened her mouth to protest. "But—"

"Enough." Arthur's growl was enough to shake the stones in the walls. "I've lost enough family. I won't put another witch or wizard in danger."

"I'm not your family," Morgan said quietly, carefully. "I'm also not a child. And one day you'll realize that."

She turned on her heel and stormed off. Arthur closed his eyes for a moment, as though he were alone. I saw the stress and strain in the bags under his eyes. The man was truly stretched to his wit's end, and this wasn't near to being over.

When he opened his eyes again, his gray gaze was calm and sure. "It's time to go."

We filed into the throne room. The knights all stood as we came in. Then we all moved to the door that would take us through the ley line.

I saw Lance catch Gwin's eyes. His gaze would usually soften for her. It didn't today. I knew why; he had every intention of taking down the man he believed violated her. The man she'd pledged to spend her life with and had apparently given a chunk of it to.

"There is a monastery about twelve miles outside of Mosul, the Mar Mattai," said Arthur.

I knew it. There was an amazing library at the monastery. It was filled with Syriac Christian manuscripts. I'd spent a few weeks pouring over the tomes a few centuries ago.

"It's on the ley line. The monks there are of an order that was allied to our cause. Gwin will stay there while we journey into the heart of Mosul to the Mosque of Yunus."

That was where we decided was the most likely place for Joseph of Arimathea to have taken the

Grail. It was an ancient temple dedicated to the biblical figure Jonah, who had been swallowed by a whale. In Joseph's poem, there had been a mention of travel by sea. It was the best lead we had, and we were running with it.

"Open the line," Arthur said to Gwin.

She stepped up and gathered the energy needed to open the ley line. The sound of the energy filled my ears as it did my veins. When I stepped through, the pounding sound didn't stop. It increased, and the ground continued to shake.

I heard someone yell for me to duck, and then I was thrown bodily to the ground. Sand and brick exploded all around me even though the energy had left. When I opened my eyes, I didn't see the walls of a temple. I didn't see a roof. The monastery was a pile of rubble, and shells rained down upon us.

CHAPTER NINETEEN

Mar Mattai was also known as Saint Matthew Monastery. The monastery was founded by Matthew in the year 361 after he fled into the mountains of the country that came to be known as Iraq. Like many religious leaders before him, Matthew had been fleeing from the persecution of the Roman Empire.

It was said that Matthew brought a knowledge of healing with him to the northern part of the country, and that he'd cured members of the royal family from life-threatening illnesses. As thanks for his service, the king fortified the monastery Matthew came to call home.

Over the ages, people came to the monastery to pay homage, to find healing, and to find peace. The monastery was a refuge in times of strife, which was a constant occurrence. I hadn't known it was built on a ley line that connected witches and wizards the world over.

Mar Mattai had been a thriving place of devotion and scholarship when I'd last visited. That was back in the twelfth century, and there had been a series of attacks and counter-attacks led by neighboring Kurds. Inside the walls of the holy place, the monks continued their daily devotions of protecting the knowledge inside, the villagers below, and the spirituality in their hearts.

Centuries later, the fighting raged on. These days, the monastery housed refugees fleeing ISIS. Those protecting the monks and their charges were the Dwek Nawsha, an Assyrian Patriotic Party, and Kurdish Peshmerga fighters. There was nothing like war to make adversaries take a closer look at the battle lines they'd drawn in the past.

Here in present day, as I rose from the blast, I turned around and looked up at the once-vibrant building. It still sat proudly on the sand-hued horizon. Its steeples stretched up toward a smoke-filled sky. Down below, the village looked like a desert ghost town.

Once upon a time, there was grass rolling down

the hills and pilgrims lining the way. It was now an overrun dirt path with crumbling stone from the church dotting here and there like decapitated flower heads.

I could see the lights from Mosul, only twelve miles away, through the hazy smoke. Oil coated my tongue as I tried to take a full breath of air. And that wasn't the worst of it.

Pieces of parchment filled the air. The paper looked old, ancient. I reached up and grabbed one. My stomach lurched as I recognized the ancient Syriac characters.

I knew what this was. It was pieces of the prized manuscripts the monks had sequestered inside. Syriac was the written form of the Syrian language, which was closely related to the Aramaic language spoken by Jesus. These documents were priceless.

I reached out my hands, trying to grab all the precious pieces of paper I could. But it was a fool's errand. They burned up and wilted in the smoke-filled air. Then another thunderous boom sent the shards out of my reach.

Fighter jets flew over our heads, leaving behind a trail of dark smoke. A second later, the sky turned orange from the mortar that had left the jet.

Red clouded my vision as the papers continued

their trickling rain shower. I took another breath, but it was once again cut short by the smoke, oil, and chemical components in the air. I turned toward the oncoming fire, tugging free one of my sais and filling my other hand with a dagger.

A small army of ISIS fighters were headed for the bottom of the hill that led up to the monastery. They wore the sandy-colored uniforms and yellow face coverings to indicate they were not the front-line soldiers. Nor were they the suicide bombers who wore all black. No. These were the elite guard— the executioners. And they were headed for the gates of the monastery.

I gripped my weapons and opened my arms for them. They were the reason for the destruction. They would pay for those lost words with their lives.

But I couldn't advance down the hill. I was shoved forward and through the gates of the temple. When I tried to fight back, to get at the real enemy, Arthur gripped my forearms, stopping the motion of my body and my blades.

"They have guns and grenades," he said. "We have swords."

I chewed over his words, my anger dying down slower than we had time for. The knights and I might survive a bullet or two, but not an array of bullets. And most likely, not a grenade. Finally, I relented and allowed him to tug me toward the monastery.

Lance had Gwin tucked into his chest. When another blast sounded, he swooped her into his arms, shielding her body with his. Loren ran in the cluster of the other knights. Arthur and I brought up the rear, his large body taking most of the dust and rocks that flew about.

"We need a tactical advantage," he said. "Maybe we can get up high in one of the towers?"

"There are secret passages for hiding in the monastery," I said. It was how many of the monks had survived over the centuries as war continuously knocked on their door.

We raced into the monastery. The doors had been left wide open, and I feared the worst. The walls were bare and the pews were empty. But off in the distance, I heard chanting.

When we came upon the men dressed in black robes with their heads bowed and their voices raised in a melodious chant, we all froze. Our sense of urgency came at odds with our manners. But only for a second. This was life or death.

I called to them in their language. They didn't raise their heads as they continued their song of praise. Outside, the sounds of war raged on. The ground shook beneath our feet. The pitter-patter of stones falling to the ground punctuated the silence that followed the end of the monks' prayer.

Finally, one male raised his dark head. Though he couldn't tell if we were friend or foe, he offered us a peaceful smile and rose. In his hands was a shiny metal object. The knights around me tensed. Lance brought Gwin behind his body. Gawain stepped in front of Loren. Arthur blocked me with one of his massive arms.

The monk brought his hands to his chest in a prayer motion. The piece of metal slipped from his fingers, and at the bottom of the chain swung a cross. A collective sigh of relief, and a sniff of chagrin, went through the knights.

"You're in danger," Arthur said. "We have to get to the highest point in the monastery."

The monk smiled. "We have been under attack for sixteen hundred years. Romans, Kurds, ISIS—the names and faces change. Only we remain. Saint Matthew and the Father will provide. They always have."

The monk turned and went to an opening in the wall. He pulled on a long rope. A bell sounded above us. But as it sounded, another blast shook the ground, drowning out the sound of the ringing and replacing it with that constant tone that vibrated the eardrum.

I went over to the window and saw that the ISIS soldiers were halfway up the hill. But not only that. In their wake came a tank. The idea of hiding out in the walls was now a moot point. A hiding spot would do us no good if the walls came tumbling down around us, blasted by the gun power of a tank.

I felt Arthur over my shoulder. The tension ran off him like hot oil.

"Can Gwin open another ley line?" I asked.

Arthur shook his head. "The way we came in is destroyed. It's too unstable to try and make another connection."

"Let me try," said Gwin. "If we can get back outside, I might be able to raise a protective shield and then open the ley line back up."

"Over my dead body will you be put in the line of fire," growled Lance. "This was supposed to be a safe place for you and it's not."

"So what do we do?" I asked, deferring to Arthur because I was out of ideas as the men in deathly yellow continued up the hill, running as though their lives depended on it.

In fact, they weren't running in any formation

that I'd seen soldiers run. They looked as though they were running from the tank, not as the advance guard of it.

They reached the top of the monastery and came face-to-face with the gates that we'd locked. A few of the enemy soldiers worked at the lock while others turned and fired on the tank. And then I saw it.

The American flag on the side of the tank.

"Praise God," said the monk who'd rung the bell.

Down below, the ISIS soldiers were laying down their arms. The tank opened, and men in the camouflage colors of the Allied Forces got out and took the enemy down.

I leaned further out the window as another dark head emerged out of the top of the tank. This man wore no soldier's uniform. He didn't look out at the ISIS soldiers. He looked up.

A tickle hit the back of my throat as my breathing went decidedly shallow. Finally, Tres found my gaze. His smile spread across his face as he waved up at the tower.

CHAPTER TWENTY

"You just can't seem to keep yourself out of trouble, can you, Dr. Rivers?" said Tres.

I walked out of the monastery as Tres swaggered into the gates. The army pants he wore hugged his thighs. The shirt tucked into his waistband showed off his narrow hips and hinted at the six-pack beneath the fabric.

"Hi, Tres." Loren wiggled her fingers. She inhaled and her breasts swelled.

I turned to her, glaring.

Her expression turned pinched and she exhaled, but her boobs were still facing the same direction, headed for Tres. Loren shrugged, completely unapologetic. Then she crossed her arms over her chest. At the approach of the military men, she uncrossed them again.

I turned back to Tres. "What are you doing here?"

"What does it look like?" he said. "Trying to get a date."

He came and stood toe to toe with me. I was a tall woman, but I had to tilt my head up to look into his dark gaze. I wasn't used to feeling small. I didn't feel small when I was around him. More like overwhelmed by the power that he exuded.

Tres was the third oldest Immortal, but he looked as though he wasn't a day over thirty at best. With his honey-golden skin, dark hair, and dark eyes, he looked like he'd walked out of his tent across the way, not out of the million-dollar condo he'd probably come from.

"When you said Sarras, I figured there were only a few places that might interest you," he continued. "When you weren't at the Mosque of the Prophet Yunus, I figured you might be here looking for the Syriac Translations."

The mention of the destroyed documents made my fingers clench. I eyed one of the ISIS soldiers, ready to take out my anger at the destruction these men had caused to these people present, past, and ancient. But that would have to be another time. There was still more work to do.

"That's actually where we're headed," I said, turning my attention back to Tres and the ride behind him. "We were on our way to the mosque. Do you think you could give us a lift?"

Half an hour later, we all piled into the tank and took off at a breakneck speed. The sounds of gunshots and explosions were muffled, but I felt the reverberations inside the metal cage.

I sat across from Tres. His long legs stretched out across the aisle. With each bump in the road, the booted toe of his shoe moved closer to mine.

"So, this is your idea of a date?" I spoke through the microphone of a headset. The inside of a tank was anything but silent. Even sitting next to someone, as we were, we still had to shout to be heard.

"No." He shook his head. "This isn't a date. It's a rescue mission. There will be no weapons present the next time I come to court you."

He cocked his head and studied me. I felt heat at each juncture where his sharp gaze rested momentarily.

"Unless...?" he hedged.

I swatted at him. He chuckled. Instead of evading

my jab, which he could've done easily, he caught my hand in his and held it.

Another bump sent his boot right up to the tip of mine. The tank swerved and the tops of our knees knocked together.

"Well," I said as he rubbed his thumb on the inside of my index finger, "this isn't so bad, as third dates go."

"This isn't our third date."

"No, I suppose not. You said I had you on your knees shortly after our original first date."

Another bump and my butt was at the edge of my seat. His face loomed over mine. And then not one, but a chorus of people cleared their throats.

Tres looked left. I looked right. We'd forgotten that we weren't alone in the tank. We also weren't the only individuals wearing headphones. Everyone had them on so that we could communicate with each other—the knights, the soldiers, Loren, and Gwin. But it appeared Tres and I had taken over the airwaves with our flirting.

He let my fingers go reluctantly and leaned back against the interior of the tank. But he didn't remove his booted foot away from mine.

"So, what are you translating here in Mosul?" asked Tres.

"What?"

"You said that's what he needed you for." Tres cocked his head toward Arthur, who lounged back in his seat.

"She translated the documents for me already." Arthur looked relaxed, but tension was in his body, as we were cooped up in a little metal box and rolling through a war zone. "She begged to tag along into a war zone. Now, I realize why."

Tres turned to glare at the Celtic king. A smug smile crossed Arthur's face. I had known that Arthur and Tres didn't get along. But I'd known that before Tres and I started getting along. So this pissing contest couldn't be about me.

Arthur had no real interest in me. He was trying to rile up Tres. But why?

"Oh, I know why," said Tres. "She was obviously trying to get away from you and your repressive regime. Like most of the women under your care."

Percival and Geraint sat on either side of Arthur. At the same moment, both men reached out a hand to hold Arthur in his seat.

"Wow, tension much?" said Loren, who sat beside Gwin.

"Mr. Mohandis dallied with a witch about a hundred years ago," Gwin said.

I turned to look at Tres.

"I returned her in better condition than when she left." Tres turned up his palms in a placating fashion. "We both have pasts, Nia."

I nodded. I wasn't upset that he'd been with another person. I had his full attention right now. But Arthur clearly hadn't forgotten the dalliance.

The tank came to a jolting stop, which sent me out of my seat and into Tres's arms. I was less than an inch from his lips. I only needed to tilt my head and I'd brush his bottom lip.

That bottom lip curved up into a wicked grin. His large hands came to my sides. I felt the heat of his palms through my layers of clothing, and I gasped. But instead of pulling me closer, he brought me up with him as he stood in a crouch. He set me on my own two feet and then stepped back, sweeping his hand before him to allow me to exit the tank first.

It took my legs a moment to work, as my brain was malfunctioning. That man continually kept me on my toes. I'd need to up my game if I were to continue to tussle with him.

Outside the tank, it was eerily quiet after the continuous pecking of bullets and shattering of explosions. When we were all assembled out of the tank, we looked at the building before us. Or what was once a building.

The Mosque of Yunus lay in rubble. It had so for many years, destroyed by ISIS as they rampaged across the country to erase history. We looked around at one another in silence, like we were mourning.

"What exactly were you looking for here?" asked Tres.

"We were looking for—"

But Arthur silenced me with a look.

"He's an architect," I said. "He could help."

"I told you before," said Arthur, "we've already looked here. We did not find what we sought."

"Did you check beneath the surface?" I asked. I learned to look deeper when it came to ancient temples of worship. There was often another layer or two just beneath the surface. "There may have been more layers to the mosque. If so, Tres is the perfect person to help us find it."

"There's a lot of energy here," said Gwin. "I can feel it coursing through my veins. I think it's here."

I turned back to Tres. "Do you know anything about this building's structure?"

"I didn't build it myself," Tres said. "But I am familiar with its design. The mosque was built on top of a Christian church that, in turn, had been built on top of two other mounds."

"So at least two other layers? Can you take us down to the lower levels?" I asked.

We left the American soldiers to keep watch and began our descent beneath the rubble. We picked over fragments of walls and passageways until Tres found a doorway that led down a narrow stair. On the third level, we entered what appeared to be a shrine.

Darkness consumed us until the knights took out those neat glowing lights. The air thinned, but that wasn't too much of a problem with my immortality and the others' magic. I looked over at Loren. She seemed to be doing just fine. Whatever little magic was in her bones was protecting her from the harsh subterranean climate.

Out before us, it looked like a maze of rooms. I was about to suggest that we split up when Gwin took the lead. Both Arthur and Lance rushed to either side of her, but neither man stopped her.

As she walked ahead of us, I caught her profile. The dazed look on her face reminded me of Igraine during one of her visions. I had no clue that, in addition to her ability to heal and cast protection spells, Gwin was a seer.

She led us to a room at the far end of the maze-like hall. The room was bare. There were the remains of what looked to be pews.

Gwin went to a bare wall at the front of the room. She placed her hands on the wall and then rested her cheek against it. When she turned her unfocused gaze to Arthur, I noted he had the same hazy look.

"It's in there," said Gwin.

"I know," Arthur said. "I feel it too."

I looked around to see that all the knights had a similar unfocused cast to their eyes. They drew their swords and shields. Together, they rushed the wall.

There was a great crash as the large men and their magic shields impacted the wall. Cracks appeared on the wall. The knights backed up, preparing to do it again.

"I'm not so sure I'd advise that," said Tres. "I don't know if that's a load-bearing wall."

But the knights didn't heed his advice. They rushed again, and the wall came crashing down around them. When the dust cleared, we saw another passageway with a closed door.

Arthur rubbed at his shoulder. He holstered his weapons and then reached out to open the door.

There was a weird glow coming from the door as though a light was on inside.

One by one, the knights filed in. I was anxious to get my turn inside to see what that light was all about. Finally, the last knight went in, and I rushed across the threshold. The first thing I saw when I came into the room was a spear sitting against the inside of the doorway.

"Is that the Spear of Destiny?" Loren asked.

"It can't be." I approached the spear. But at the last minute, Lance caught my hand.

"Don't touch that," he said.

"You don't really believe it's *the* spear?" I said.

He didn't answer. I gave the object another glance. It looked like a simple wooden stick and a spearhead. There were no adornments. Nothing on it said "here lies the Spear of Destiny, which did pierce the flesh of Jesus."

When Lance turned his back, I reached out like a curious child and touched the tip. When the blade nicked me, I pulled my hand away in pain. There was blood at the tip of my finger. It should not have broken my skin so easily. I'd been around Tres for less than an hour. The effects of the allergy should not be in play yet. But not only did I bleed, I hurt.

"I said don't touch." Lance shook his head. "Magic is dangerous if you're not a witch."

"It's magic?" I asked.

"It's an object of worship that has spent hundreds of years on a ley line."

"It's a magical wound," Gwin said. "It won't heal on its own. Here, let me—"

But I walked past her into the room, my mouth agape as my finger continued to bleed. The light was coming from a casket in the center of the room. But I walked past those more interested in the treasures all around.

On the walls were depictions of the last supper of Christ that had to be hundreds, maybe even over a thousand, years old. There was furniture in the corners. Baskets open with clothing, tattered over time. Jewelry lay on tables and inside open chests. It looked like the inside of an Egyptian royal's tomb. Then I remembered that Joseph of Arimathea had been an Egyptian.

Was this his tomb?

Lined up against the wall were a series of cups. I made my way over to them, bending down to study them to try to discern which could be the Grail. I expected Arthur to displace me at any moment, but he didn't come near. In fact, I didn't see him looming anywhere near me.

I stood up and noticed for the first time that the casket, from where the room got its light source, was actually a sarcophagus. But in the tomb, there was no mummy. There was no man. I gasped at the sight of the body in the tomb.

The items in this room could easily be older than five hundred years, likely closer to one or two thousand. Even in this underground tomb, the wear of age had made a visible effect. But the woman in the casket looked as though she were only sleeping.

The woman was old, but she'd aged well. Her salt-and-pepper hair was spread out before her. Her ruby lips didn't part in a sigh, but they looked as though she would open them at any moment with a delicate yawn. Her hands were crossed at her chest, the nails still neatly trimmed. She looked as though she'd just lain down for an afternoon nap. But for centuries upon centuries.

"Who is she?" I asked, but was met with silence.

Every knight in the room was on his knee, bowing before the woman. Even Gwin was prostrate.

Arthur straightened and approached the reposing woman as though fearful he'd awaken her from her sleep. "This is Joseph's wife, Mary de

Marmore. More commonly known as Mary Magdalene."

My eyes widened as I took in the woman again. I had met her. But that was over two thousand years ago. She'd been a devout follower of Jesus at the time. She'd also been his family by marriage.

"She was a witch," said Gwin. "A powerful one. Who has been laid to rest on a ley line. The magic doesn't die, remember? It lives on until it's returned to the source."

"She is the Grail," I said.

It all made sense now. Hugues de Payins had written the letter to his father, Joseph. History had told that after the death of Christ, one of his followers had taken Mary Magdalene to Europe. She and her family eventually settled in France. That follower of Jesus had been his uncle, Joseph of Arimathea. Joseph was the husband of Mary Magdalene.

Part of me wanted to jump for joy at such a find. The other part kept calculating the meaning of a two-thousand-year-old witch lying in a pool of supernatural light. That light wasn't made of electricity or phosphorous. It was pure magic.

"You're going to burn her?" I asked.

"We have to," Gwin said. "If we don't, her magic could fall into the wrong hands."

"Why didn't her husband do it?" I asked.

"Joseph was Egyptian," said Arthur. "Neither he nor Lady Mary practiced the ritual of burning. And he loved my great-grandmother too much to see her body harmed in any way. So he hid her away from us."

"Your great-grandmother?" I asked.

"Mary Magdalene de Marmor's daughter, my grandfather's wife, was called Mara. History called her Marlin or Merlin."

My head was spinning. Arthur was the descendant of Mary Magdalene and the uncle of the Virgin Mary, Joseph of Arimethea. That was why Queen Mara had always looked so familiar to me. I'd known her family. It was too much to take in.

"She's the chalice," I said. "Her body is the Holy Grail. And the two angels in the poem? They were her children." Lady Merida and Joseph de Paganis, better known to history as Hugues de Payens.

Arthur nodded. "For centuries, Joseph and Lady Mary helped my family in the crusade to protect magical kind. But their son was born without magic, and he resented it. He gave rise to our greatest enemies, the Knights Templar."

"And now we have to burn her body before the Templars find her," said Lance.

"Resentment, I think, is too strong a word," came a voice from the entryway. "Perhaps our dear cousin was only trying to even the mortal odds in an unfair magical world."

CHAPTER TWENTY-ONE

The metallic clanging and air-splitting whoosh of swords being raised filled the air. But as soon as they were raised, they were lowered like dead weight when the knights were confronted with the man standing in the entryway.

Merlin stood before us in robes. He'd been a tall, lanky giant as a youth. His cheeks had always been gaunt, never quite filling out. His chest, even through his tunics, had always appeared sunken in when he stood next to his brother or another of the knights. He'd always looked to me like a child wearing a warrior's body.

Merlin looked ancient now. His dark hair was snow white. The facial hair that had never come for him in Camelot now extended down his chest as a downy beard of wisps. He only needed the pointy cap to complete the look of the Disney cartoon character that bore his name. Merlin was older than every knight present, and now he looked like a seventy-year-old man. The quarter-century that he'd been away from his homeland and off the ley line had not been kind to him.

"Merlin?"

I heard Gwin's voice, but I didn't see her. Lance had her blocked behind his large body. His arms stretched back, not allowing her to pass. He was also the only knight who still had his sword raised, ready to attack.

Merlin's dark eyes paid his wife no heed. His gaze was fastened on the body in the sarcophagus. "She's here."

His voice was paper-thin. It didn't croak and creek like an old man's. His voice had always been soft.

"I had begun to doubt I would ever find her," he continued as he slow-marched into the room. His body moved as though it too were weighed down by the hands of time. "I'd searched this temple before and felt her presence, but I couldn't find her. Not until you led her to me, my dear."

It was clear that he spoke to Gwin, but still he

didn't take his eyes off Lady Mary's reposed body.

"Even now, you're still taking care of me. With Lady Mary's magic inside of me, I will have all the strength I will ever need."

Merlin took another step. Before he could reach for the casket, Arthur stepped between its contents and his brother, sword raised, face set in a grim line.

Merlin's gaze slowly focused on his younger brother. The steel of the sword glinted in his dark eyes. "You would kill your own brother?"

"It looks as though you've already done that," said Arthur. "I don't see my blood. I see a madman, a murderer. You've taken the lives of those we're all sworn to protect."

Merlin shook his head. The puffs of his hair looked like clouds cast around his head. "I did what was necessary to survive, as we have always done. As you and our father and his father before him taught us. We put the good of the people ahead of ourselves."

Arthur's jaw worked at having his words thrown back in his face, but so out of context. "You've killed your own kind, sucked the life out of them in your quest to save your own life. That is not chivalry. That is cowardice."

"I didn't take their lives," said Merlin. "I brought

them to glory, baptized them under the Word of our Lord. I told you, I heard the voice of God. He sent me one of his messengers. He said to surrender. That God is the One and I am his prophet. Those witches didn't submit to the Word, and their lives became forfeit."

"No." Gwin's voice was part sob, part plea. "This isn't who you are. You have a good soul."

Merlin looked over at her for the first time. "A good soul? But a weak body. Not a full man, was it?"

"I never said that," Gwin cried, her face contorted in a mix of horror, guilt, and sorrow.

"You didn't have to." Merlin's eyes latched onto Lance, who still shielded Gwin with his large body. "You gave me your strength, my life. It was you who taught me to see the light, the way."

"I never hurt you and you never hurt me," insisted Gwin. "You don't have to hurt anyone now. Not anymore. Let me help you. Like I used to. I have plenty to give."

"I no longer need your pity." Merlin's eyes fastened to Mary Magdalene lying sedate in the coffin. "Like you, I have found another. The Holy Grail. Mother Mary's power has been resting quietly on the ley line thanks to her husband's sentimentality."

With a signal from Arthur, the knights pulled rank around the body of the ancient witch.

Merlin sighed. "No one has to die tonight. Just submit to me, surrender your power, and you too will find his glory."

"I already have a date with death," said Gawain. "And it ain't tonight."

"It's over, Merlin," said Arthur.

"Oh, brother, it's only just begun. You think I am still the weakling you all pitied when you were children. But I am strong now. I am the way, the light."

Merlin opened his hand. Arthur's eyes widened, and I saw him grit his teeth. His sword arm began to shake. The veins popped out as he gripped the sword first with one and then with a second hand. But his fingers peeled off and the sword flew through the air, straight into Merlin's magical grasp.

The knights' faces went lax at the sight of Excalibur in the hand of another. Arthur's hands hung limp at his sides as he eyed his greatest weapon in the hand of his brother.

"Our kind have been persecuted for ages," said Merlin. "But I've seen the light. The true followers will get to the Father through me."

Merlin raised his free hand. I could feel the

energy swell in the room. I felt my own sai wiggle in my hand. I tried to tighten my hold, but the blood still leaking from my finger made my grip loose. Then my weapon was yanked away.

It rose vertically, then came to lie flat, right at my throat. One look around the room showed that every sword was pointed at its owner's throat. Including Excalibur at Arthur's.

"I was once weak," said Merlin. "But now am strong. Was blind, but now I see. Amazing is His grace."

From the corner of my eye, I saw Lance palm a dagger. He reached up with the smaller weapon and parried his sword, striking it hard enough that the blade was blown to the side. The small amount of room gave him a way forward, and he charged Merlin.

Merlin pointed his finger at Lance, and the knight was lifted into the air off his feet.

"You think you are righteous in this action?" said Merlin. "But you've broken our Lord's covenant. You have coveted my wife for decades. For your sins, you shall feel my wrath."

Lance's body was thrown like a rag doll into the wall. A scream tore through the room. It was Gwin as she looked at the knight's crumpled body. She took a step toward Lance, but her body froze in motion.

With a wave of his hand, Merlin set Gwin's feet toward him. It was clear that she fought his hold on her. But Merlin's magic was dark and twisted. Gwin and the other witches hadn't been trained in combat. Gwin knew only how to heal and shield those she cared about.

"I did love you," Merlin said as he brought her before him. "I did not start to truly live until the moment you were born. I knew you were meant for me the moment I felt the strength of your magic. And you will be a part of me forever."

I had been inside the rituals of the Greeks where they took the souls of their Devoted. That had been a heady experience, an offering from a Chosen human to a powerful god. I had also been present when souls were ripped from humans' unwilling bodies. During that sacrilege, the air had been muggy and dense.

As Merlin began to claim Gwin's magic, it felt as though the air was being sucked out of the room. And we were all helpless to do anything. The swords at our throats pressed on.

As her body arched back from the taking, Gwin's head turned. Her eyes connected with mine. Her gaze dipped to my bleeding hand. I saw her gulp. She shut her eyes briefly. Then they turned back to her husband. Her voice when she spoke was a strained whisper.

"I would've given my soul if you had asked."

She opened her hand. The Spear of Destiny flew up from its place at the entryway and came to her. Then the woman of peace, the woman who healed the wounds of others, the woman who had given part of her soul to her husband, thrust the blade into Merlin's side.

His eyes widened, and he let her go. They both fell to the floor. So did the spear. So did all the weapons aimed at our necks.

Loren was closest to Gwin, and she went to her. Gawain went to Lance. Arthur reached for his sword and pointed it at his bleeding brother. The spear had only pierced the fabric and the skin of Merlin's side, but he was bleeding profusely. Before Arthur could say a word to offer mercy or raise his sword to deliver a final blow, the sound of a dozen safeties being released rang throughout the tomb.

We looked up to find the entryway filled with ISIS soldiers and Knights Templar. But it was the man standing amid the soldiers who made me gasp and clutch for my weapons.

"Tisa, why am I not surprised to see you here? Wherever there is crumbling rubble, there you are trying to save it. Ah, and you're with Horus this century."

"What are you doing here, Yod?"

"Why, my life's work, of course."

There were at least a dozen military-grade guns pointed in the room, held by the ISIS soldiers and Templars alike. I shuddered to think what had happened to our military escort outside.

Yod stepped out in front of his two squads of religious zealots. His blond curls were tucked under a military-style cap. He wore dark fatigues over his honeyed skin. His dark blue eyes looked soulless as he eyed Tres and me. He wasn't as old as Tres, but the impact of two other Immortals in close proximity sent a wave of nausea wafting through my head.

I had made it a point to steer clear of Yod for more reasons than just the allergy. He held very little value for human life. He had no problem mowing down an entire civilization if it would suit his end. They didn't know it, but these soldiers were just nameless, faceless pawns in his efforts.

Now I knew who the messenger Merlin spoke of was. I could also imagine what the message had been. It was Yod's M.O. He'd been doing this for centuries—picking off one member of a group and raising them above the status of all others only to divide the group and then conquer everyone.

"It looks like you've done the job for me already." Yod bent down to peer at Merlin, who still clutched at his bloodied side. The wizard groaned and held out his hand to Yod. Yod sighed in clear disappointment. "Only halfway done, then."

Merlin frowned, staring at Yod in confusion. "You are forsaking me?"

I could only shake my head at the situation. History had a habit of repeating itself, and it was doing it again here. I honestly wasn't sure if there was a God. But if there was, I knew for certain that someone as soulless and diabolical as Yod would not be their messenger.

"But I am the chosen of God," Merlin insisted, still not getting that he was a pawn in a larger plan.

Merlin, it would seem, was just another whom Yod led to believe was a prophet. And now that Yod was done with him, and Merlin's people sufficiently divided and weakened, Yod could pick off the rest of the magical community. We'd all played right into his hands.

Yod chuckled. "You were just another false prophet, claiming to be a Messiah."

"But God spoke to me," Merlin insisted, his voice growing weaker as his life essence continued to seep into the fabric of his robes.

"Likely a side effect of the poison running through your veins," said Yod. "What you erroneously call magic. Just like all the other false prophets had been touched by the same affliction. It's a plague amongst mankind. Death is the only cure."

I had never known why Yod had such a hatred toward the religious and spiritual giants of mankind. Now it was becoming clear. He believed they were all descendants of witches. I had never made the connection, but thinking on it now, he may have a point. Warped though it was.

Joseph of Arimathea, the uncle of Jesus's mother, came from a magical line. There was a mention of the Prophet Mohammed in Hindu scriptures that, now that I thought about it, could be interpreted that he had magical blood when it stated that he would be given protection against his enemies. If I thought long and hard about it, I could make a connection that most spiritual leaders of the last few millennia had a connection to magic. I just didn't have time to think about it right now, not with zealots pointing guns at my body and an insane Immortal in charge of the triggers.

Instead, I decided to state the obvious, to keep Yod talking, as I worked out a way to get us all out of this. "You killed all the great prophets of human spirituality—Jesus, Mohammed, Siddartha."

"Of course," said Yod. "We can't have false prophets running around the world detracting from the truth."

"What truth?"

"Have you forgotten?" He smiled at me. "These humans need to believe there is a Heaven and a Hell, an almighty God looking out for them, but we know the truth. Don't we?"

Yod looked between Tres and me. Then he reached down and grabbed a handful of blonde hair. I took a step forward, but Tres held me back as Loren screamed with Yod's grip around her locks.

Loren reached up and clawed at Yod's hand to no avail. Even with two other Immortals present, the impact of her nails would barely reach his notice. He pulled a dagger from his utility belt and held it at her throat.

"Man's weakness," he continued, "has always been woman. Since Eve, on to Mary, and then Guinevere." He peered into Loren's blue eyes, so like her cousin's. Gwin was on her knees, looking up helplessly as we all stared down the barrels of a dozen guns. "Females tempt us with fruits so sweet that they leave a bitter taste when they leave."

I could taste the bile in my throat as I saw Loren's neck strain in his grasp. Her eyes connected with mine, and my hand itched for one of the daggers in my boot. But I knew the sharp blade would do no good against Yod and his Immortal body.

Yod came to the sarcophagus, dragging Loren alongside him. His hands hovered over the reposed body of Mary Magdalene. "They say she was the greatest of her kind."

Then he turned to me.

"Are you here for the Grail, Tisa? Did you think it was a cup? You were always so literal." He chuckled. "No, this artifact is better than any tin cup. It's a pristine witch's body filled to the brim with magical energy."

"What are you going to do with her?" I asked.

"Destroy the body, of course. Then kill this witch." He jerked Loren. "And the knights. Magic is a scourge. Behind every notable prophet has been a witch. When they are all gone, mankind will only look toward one god."

The soldiers behind him most certainly thought he meant their god, but I knew that Yod thought of himself as a god. I also knew there was nothing I could do to convince those men that just as Merlin lay on the floor after his usefulness had run out, their bodies would soon be trampled under Yod's heel. They weren't my first concern. Loren was.

"The only time there was peace in this world," said Yod, "was after the flood. When they all were wiped away. Not everyone will get into the garden. There must be sacrifices."

The garden? Sacrifice?

"And now that I have all the Knights of the Round Table, their great wizard, and their strongest witch, I can pick off the rest of them. Then the world will be rid of magic."

He looked to Tres and me as though waiting for our approval.

"We are the true prophets," said Yod. "Humans should follow our word. That's why we're here. To save humanity from sin."

"Excuse me," Loren said. "Mr. Crazy Immortal guy?"

I wanted to wring her neck myself to shut her up, because I didn't have a clue how to handle this situation. I needed more time to keep working on a plan of escape. I didn't need her stepping in with her snark.

"Do you think I could get a last word before you, you know, off with my head?"

Yod frowned down at her.

"Okay," said Loren. "All I want to say is that nothing can shield me from my destiny."

The room was silent except for the sound of running water. I noticed for the first time that there was a stream somewhere in the ground. I could hear the running liquid as it made its way through the rocks as it, too, puzzled out what the heck Loren was trying to say.

She sighed and repeated her words. "Nothing

can *shield* me"—she stared pointedly at Gwin —"from my *destiny*." She stared pointedly at me when she emphasized the word *destiny*.

Then she looked up to Yod.

"Okay," she said. His grip had loosened slightly. "I'm ready. On three, okay?"

The knights around us had pinched expressions as their fingers twitched, eager to go into action, but helpless with the weapons trained on them. The soldiers were at a standstill, waiting for Yod to give them an order.

Yod stared, completely befuddled, at the woman he thought was the Lady Guinevere. But I had gotten her meaning. I only hoped Gwin did, too. Otherwise, this would be a bust.

"One," Loren began. And then, "Wait, we're going *on* three, okay? One, two, three—"

Loren kicked at the Spear of Destiny, which lay at Merlin's side. The staff flew up into the air and landed in my hand. I aimed it for Yod's chest now that Loren had shifted into his side. The blade of the spear struck true. Yod's eyes opened wide in shock and his hand released Loren. But they both tumbled to the ground.

The sound of bullets filled the air. But none of them struck us. With everyone's attention on the spectacle Loren had created, Gwin was able to raise a shield of protection around us.

The knights quickly moved into action. Their magical swords could penetrate Gwin's shield, and they picked off the Templars and soldiers with ease.

I ran to Loren. She lay face down across Yod's body. Yod lay with his eyes opened wide and his lips parted as he gulped down air with wet gasps.

"Nia?"

I looked down at Loren and gagged. Her brown shirt had turned a dark maroon. Across her chest was a gash where Yod's dagger had struck her. The gaping wound was deep and would need more than a surgeon to heal.

CHAPTER TWENTY-THREE

"No," I said as I grasped her by her shoulders. Loren's head lolled back as her lips parted. Her eyes fluttered and then opened wide.

For a moment, my brain was distracted by the fact that she was wearing my shirt. The expensive fabric was torn in two like the fashion of the eighties where shirts and pants and even skirts sported gashes and distressed looks.

The tear on Loren's flesh was no fashion statement. It was a death sentence.

It had been inevitable. Since the first day we'd met on the steps of the Museum of the American Indian. She'd come down the steps in a Stella

McCartney skirt with a call to adventure in her hands.

I'd walked away from her that day, but I'd known in my heart that it wasn't over. She'd been hogtied the first adventure she'd gone on with me, literally. She'd had her soul taken the second time, literally. And now, for the third time, her heart was in my hands, literally.

I pushed at her chest, trying to stave off the blood flow. But her life's essence continued to seep out of her. Her breathing was ragged and her body trembled.

"No," I whispered. Then I shouted it out. But there was no deity to answer my prayer. As I looked back down at my best friend, Loren smiled.

"Hey," she said, her voice croaking. "Don't say I didn't have your back."

I nodded. "Now I've got yours." I brought her bleeding chest to mine, wishing that the beating of my heart was enough to heal hers.

"I'm gonna die, aren't I?"

"No." I shook my head in full denial as I held her close.

"I need to ask you for something," Loren said, her voice scratchy. "It's really important and you can't get mad, okay?"

"Anything. Name it."

Her gaze slid off me and landed on something just over my shoulder. Tres stood at my back, dagger drawn even though not a single enemy stood. The sounds of bullets and grunts of death had stopped. The Templars and soldiers were all down. Only the knights remained, and they all stood in a protective circle around Loren.

"I love you and all, but do you mind if he holds me?" Loren asked. Her gaze was directed at Tres. "If I can't live like a billionairess, at least I can pretend I'll die like one."

"No," I said.

Loren closed her eyes with a wince. "Cock blocker."

"You're not dying." I looked around, my eyes wide. Then I saw Loren's virtual twin standing over us. "Gwin. Help."

Gwin sank down to the ground on the other side of Loren. Her face was a torment of sorrow. "There's too much blood," she said. "I can't heal this."

I shook my head. "You have to do something. She can't die."

"There's nothing..." But then she stopped. Gwin looked up at the body lying in the sarcophagus.

Mary Magdalene continued her deathly

slumber, completely undisturbed by the destruction wrought around her. Her body still glowed with the magic that filled her, the magic that would never die unless burned in ritual. Or siphoned and poured into another living witch.

I turned to Gwin. She chewed at her bottom lip with uncertainty. I set my mouth in a determined line.

"No," Arthur said.

I ignored his command. "Do it," I said to Gwin. "Do it now."

"What you ask her to do is dark magic," Arthur protested. "It's what began this series of events in the first place."

"We'd all be dead if it wasn't for Loren."

Arthur's jaw was locked in dissent.

"She's your family," I insisted.

I looked around at the knights. There was uncertainty on many of their faces.

"She's *my* family," I pleaded.

Gawain came up to Arthur and put a hand on his shoulder. "It may be the only way to contain Lady Mary's magic. If we burn her body as is customary, the magic will seep into the lines of this place. There's too much strife here for this amount of magic to roam uncontained."

Arthur looked around the room at his knights. Their faces showed a mixture of sorrow, indecision, and wavering compassion as they looked down at Loren's shivering, mangled body.

"He has a point," said Lance, who came to stand beside me. He clutched at his side where he'd impacted the wall.

I heard Gwin gasp at Lance's acquiescence, but he did not meet her eye.

Finally, Arthur turned back to me, looked down at Loren, and then glanced over at Gwin. He gave a single nod of his head.

I looked down at Loren. Her eyes were closed, and it didn't look as though she was breathing anymore. My heart stopped to think I may have already lost her, that I'd spent her last moments arguing with a bunch of men instead of giving her my full attention.

That bunch of men came and scooped her lifeless body out of my arms. I had to fight to keep my fingers from grasping her to me. They held her near the sarcophagus as Gwin began a chant.

I stayed where I was on the floor. My body slumped backward, but I didn't hit the dirt. A strong chest met my back. I let my head come to rest beneath Tres's chin. I couldn't see what they were doing to my friend. The magic buzzing through the room calmed me. The magic and Tres's heart beating against my back lulled me into a feeling that everything was going to be okay.

I watched the family of knights and witch above me as they worked to save one of their own. Arthur oversaw the ritual like the commander that he was. Even though he barely knew Loren, he would do everything he could to ensure that the granddaughter of Sir Galahad made it through this.

I watched as Gawain cradled her head and Lance held her feet. Sweat poured off Gwin's forehead as she worked her magic. It warmed me to know that Loren wasn't alone. I was glad that she had found people like her in the world, people who would go to bat for her.

I wondered if they would afford the same to Merlin. I turned in Tres's arms to check on the fallen wizard. But the ground where he'd fallen was empty.

I straightened a bit and looked harder. It was easy to make out the fallen forms of the ISIS soldiers in yellow camouflage and the Templars in black and red. But there was no Merlin.

"He's gone."

"Who?" asked Tres.

I put my feet under me and stood slowly. Tres

came up beside me. Merlin must have gotten away as we all turned our attention to Loren. As a wizard, he would've been able to get out of Gwin's protective shield, even with the wound from the Spear of Destiny.

I wondered if his magic was capable of healing the wound that Gwin had given him with the spear. We'd have to go and look for Merlin at some point. Both he and Yod were deranged in their beliefs. Merlin couldn't be left to roam free.

Neither could Yod. But I had no idea how we'd contain him. Immortals had never had cause to imprison one another, but Yod's intentions to wreak genocidal havoc on the magical community had to come to an end.

I turned to find him still lying on the ground where he'd fallen, still as a statue. The blood had stopped seeping out of the wound in his chest, but it gaped open even wider. Wounds increased their size when the object that had pierced them was pulled out.

The object that had caused Yod's injury, the Spear of Destiny, was nowhere to be found.

"Merlin must have taken the spear," I said.

Tres didn't respond. He bent down over Yod. He reached his hand to Yod's neck, likely looking for a pulse. I frowned at the move. Yod was Immortal. The spear would only maim him. It couldn't kill him.

I swiped my hair away from my head. I felt the slipperiness of my finger, which still bled from nicking the tip of the spear, the magical spear that had killed one of the greatest spiritual teachers the world had ever known, the magical spear which had spent hundreds of years on a ley line while people all around the world revered its fabled abilities.

I turned back to Tres. His eyes were wide as he looked from Yod to me.

"He's dead," said Tres.

Dead? But my lips wouldn't work to ask Tres to repeat himself.

Yod was dead? A couple of months ago, I would've said it was impossible. Immortals didn't die. But Vau and Epsilon's lives had been taken. Now Yod?

Twelve were exiled. Only seven will return.

Yod had said, *Not everyone will get into the garden. There must be sacrifices.*

And now he was gone too, leaving behind nine. Which, if Igraine's prophecy was true, meant that two more Immortals were going to die.

CHAPTER TWENTY-FOUR

My hands shook as I dialed the number. Even though my fingers trembled, the face of my phone stayed clear as I pressed each of the numbers I knew by heart. My finger had stopped bleeding after Gwin had reached out for my hand to heal me. There had been nothing she could do for Yod. We'd burned his lifeless body along with Lady Mary's before we left the tomb and went back into the war zone.

Now, I sat huddled in the corner of my room in the bowels of Tintagel back in Camelot. My phone rang and rang in my ear. The voice message recording came on, and my heart arrested in my chest. I took a couple of deep breaths, hit *end*, and dialed again.

I told myself not to freak out as the ring tone shuddered down my eardrum, shivered over my shoulders, and trembled down my spine.

An Immortal was dead. A delusional wizard was on the loose. At his disposal was a weapon that had taken the lives of gods.

The Spear of Destiny had been used to pierce Jesus. I wasn't sure if it had been the final cause of his death, but his followers' belief that it had been the death knell, coupled with the fact that the weapon had sat on a ley line for hundreds of years, imbued the item with enough magic to do the job to any supernatural creature that walked the earth.

And Merlin could be anywhere. He could be planning anything. He'd seen what the spear could do. There was nothing stopping him from going on a rampage and killing witches, wizards, gods, and Immortals.

And still the phone rang on unanswered. I had to face facts. No one would answer on the other end.

It was getting close to voice message territory. What would I say on the recording? *There's a crazy wizard with a spear of death who could be gunning for you.* Like he'd believe—

"*Oui?*"

The sound through the receiver was like a gale

wind battering the side of a ship. It rocked me back, and the back of my head hit the wall from its force and its bite.

Zane's voice was curt. Even when he was angry with me, he was never curt. But I couldn't force any words out of my mouth. I was so happy to hear his voice, even if it was just that one sharp word. He could've hung up the phone, he could've told me to go to hell, he could've said nothing at all. All I cared about was that he was okay.

It had been an irrational fear—that Merlin would go after him. But I had been through too much these past couple of days, these past couple of weeks. I wasn't thinking clearly.

This was the first time that I'd sat still, the first time I'd been alone, truly by myself, and my first instinct had been to reach out to him. This was the first time ever that he didn't reach back for me.

My breaths came out fast and shallow. Tears streamed down my face as everything came crashing down on me. I wrapped my arms around my body as a low, keening wail escaped my lips.

"Nova?"

His tone lost its bite. The strong wind whose tendrils had slapped the breath out of me was replaced by a cool breeze meant to soothe my hurts.

It wrapped around me like an ocean breeze coming ashore after a rocky voyage. The softness of his voice made me sob openly.

I was thankful he couldn't see me. Because it was an ugly cry. Had I been wearing mascara, it would've been streaming down my cheeks. My eyes, I was sure, were blotchy. My bottom lip trembled. I didn't bother sniffing back the snot that wanted to journey to my upper lip.

"*Où es-tu*," he said. "Nova, please. Tell me, where are you?"

His voice was urgent, tinged with fear. I understood the feeling all too well. I was one of those women who never cried. Stiff upper lip Nia, that was me. But I sobbed into the receiver like a baby.

I took a couple of deep breaths until I could say words steadily. I had to explain to him that my tears were ones of relief. "I'm safe."

I took a few more deep breaths. He remained silent while I got myself together. It was an impossible feat since I was a wreck.

Loren was not doing so well. She was alive thanks to Lady Mary's magic fueling her magical soul. But her wound wasn't healing as it should. She hadn't woken up since we'd gotten back to Caerleon this morning.

I didn't tell Zane any of that. I didn't play on his sympathies like he'd accused me of doing back in Greece. I just needed a moment to be...well, human. And despite what we were going through at the moment, there was no one in the world that I trusted with my vulnerabilities more than Zane.

I had lost his trust. Our intimate relationship was a bust. Our friendship was in tatters. There were too many pieces to try and mend.

I could live without his affection. Probably.

I could stand him not talking to me or wanting to be around me. Mostly.

But I was certain I couldn't stand to be in this world if he wasn't in it as well, even if he hated me.

Twelve were exiled. Only seven will return.

Nine of us remained. Zane would not be one of the five to be sacrificed.

"Yod's dead," I said.

"Dead?"

I gave him a moment to process that single word. He knew that death amongst Immortals was possible. He'd been my savior when I'd nearly been murdered. Twice.

"How?" he asked.

"Magic," I said.

I didn't tell him it was by my own hand. I hadn't meant to kill Yod, only to maim him and give my friend a chance to get out of harm's way. I wasn't sorry that he was dead. His plans to ruin and rule the world would easily rank him in the top five villains ever to walk the earth. But I was afraid of what his death meant for the rest of us.

"We're all in danger," I said. "I just...I just needed to make sure you were safe."

"I am."

"There's more..." But I didn't know how to tell him about Igraine's prophecy. I didn't fully understand it myself. "Zane? Do you remember a garden?"

I shook my head, knowing I wasn't being clear. We had been alive for thousands of years. Of course he had been in many gardens. I was asking him to remember a place that I wasn't even sure about.

"My first memory of you was in a garden," he said. "You were in a field of flowers unlike anything I've ever seen. They were a deeply hued purple and a saturation of pink that I've never seen again in any land I've traveled. I don't remember where we were. I think it may be my first memory."

The flowers in my vision as I'd ridden across

Caerleon on horseback had been like that. Was the place I'd seen real?

As Immortals, we shed most of our memories. We had to in order to keep our brains functioning. No one and nothing, not even a library, could manage the amount of information we had witnessed. But Zane had once told me that he remembered everything about me, that those were the memories worth keeping.

"It was the first time that I knew that I..." he said, and then sighed.

His voice had been so soft, so reverent. Zane didn't put much stock in the words *I love you*. He whispered prayers in my ear when we made love. His words were filled with reverence, with worship. That was the tone he'd taken before he'd paused.

"The first time that you knew what?" I said.

He took a deep breath. I could hear him press his lips together, readying them to form words. I pressed the receiver closer to my ear. Then the door opened.

"Nia?" Tres's booming voice filled the small space. "There you are."

Tres walked into the room. Static rose on the line of the phone. The allergy that kept Immortals from spending too much time around one another also transferred to technology. With the two of us in such close proximity, coupled with my connection to Zane via satellite towers, the cell phone connection would not survive.

But I knew Zane was still on the line. I felt him through the ether. Felt him drifting away from me. The worst part was that I couldn't even reach out to him.

I saw the wave rising between us. Felt the waters pushing at my body as they pulled at his. I heard the whitecaps crash down on me, pushing us further apart than we had ever been.

"*Merci* for the warning." Zane's voice was terse. His tone was strained. And then, with a click, the line went dead.

I closed my eyes and let the receiver slide down my face. I felt as though I were being held underwater. My limbs were heavy and my movements sluggish.

When I finally opened my eyes, Tres was looking just past my shoulder, his mouth set in a grim line. He knew who I'd been talking to. He nodded and turned on his heel, but I reached out for him from my place on the floor.

"Please don't go," I begged.

I grasped onto his pant leg. He turned and looked down at me. I was sure I looked pathetic on my knees, hanging onto him. But I couldn't be alone right now.

The moment the phone line went dead, I felt myself falling apart. I couldn't hold myself together. I needed someone to wrap their arms around me.

Tres took a step back into the room and toward me. He slid his big body down the wall. His legs were so long that when he bent his knees, they came up to my face. His arms went behind my back. I laid my head on his shoulder. He rested his chin at my temple. His other arm came around me, and he held me tightly.

I curled into him and held on as though my life depended on it, breathing in his familiar scent. I recognized the pattern of his heartbeat. I let myself sink into him. My guard slipped. Defenses lowered all the way down. My upper lip stayed stiff as I took his comfort, and I didn't cry.

CHAPTER TWENTY-FIVE

"Nia, lookit!"

Loren snapped her fingers, and a blue flame appeared. She laughed with glee. Then, like too much gas on a pilot, the flame flared out of control. Morgan waved her hands, and the flame immediately extinguished.

Once the flame was safely out, I flew to the bed Loren was fluffed up in and threw my arms around her.

"Oof," she groaned as she took my impact.

"Oh, no." I immediately reared back. "Did I hurt you?"

The front of her nightgown gaped open, showing the faint scar on her chest.

"No, I'm good as new. Better than new. That was

just a lot of Nia for a girl to take after facing death."

Loren had faced death. Hopefully for the last time in a long time. With the witch blood that flowed in her veins from her mother's side, she could live happily and healthily for hundreds of years. Now with the magic of one of the oldest and most powerful witches to ever live running through her veins, Loren was nearly immortal.

"What?" She frowned at me. "Why are you looking at me like I'm some sort of Frankenstein?"

"Oh god." I sighed. "What have we done?"

Loren now had the strength of a knight from the blood of Galahad, along with the magic of a witch, the expertise of a forger, and the cunning of a thief.

I turned to Arthur, who stood in the doorway of her bedroom. "She's going to be a handful."

"Don't worry," he said. "She's not going anywhere."

Loren snorted. "Dude, you are *so* not the boss of me."

Beside her, Morgan's eyes twinkled. I recognized the same glint that was in Loren's eyes. It looked like that spark of mischief was a family affair.

"You're a full-blooded witch now; you have to stay here under the knights' protection," said Arthur. "Only we can keep you safe."

"Yeah, I don't do cages," Loren replied.

"You're my responsibility now."

"Oh, yeah? Where were you when my mother died? Or when my father died? I've been on my own for years and doing just fine."

"Things are different now," Arthur stated. "Once my brother learns where Lady Mary's magic went, he'll be after you. And he has the Spear of Destiny. No one's safe until we find him."

"Jeez, Nia, now I know how you felt when people were trying to suck out your bones. But still, this whole 'women stay home and men go out and fight' thing—not my cup of tea."

"Wait a minute," Morgan said. "She's of the Galahad line. And she holds the sword. It chose her. Doesn't that mean she could take the seat?"

Arthur looked aghast.

"What seat?" Loren asked.

"The seat of Sir Galahad," said Morgan, sounding gleeful. "To sit at the Round Table with the other knights."

"Don't be ridiculous, Morgan." Arthur sounded cross. "She's a woman. No woman ever has taken a seat at the table."

"She's not a woman, she's a witch," said Morgan, her tone mocking. "A witch who's been wielding the blade of her line for years with no training. You're duty-bound to train her. At least to send her through the trials. Tradition demands it."

"This is preposterous," Arthur said.

"Sir Galahad?" said Loren. "Sounds kinda cool."

I pulled Arthur to the side before he blew a blood vessel. "If she gets hurt, or if you hurt her feelings, I will use my blade on your balls. And it won't be pleasant."

Arthur looked like he was going to be sick, but I doubted it was from my words. His gaze was fixed on Loren and Morgan with their heads together on the far end of the room. He shook his head and then left.

Morgan picked up Loren's tray and, with a wink, followed Arthur out, likely to torture him a bit more. I turned to my bestie. I had always known she'd leave me. I was thankful that it wasn't in a casket.

"You're leaving?" she asked.

I nodded. "I've got to go handle something with my own kind."

I wasn't sure why I didn't tell her about Igraine's vision. What if I was one of the final two who would die in order for the remaining seven to reenter this garden paradise? If that were true, I didn't want her worrying about me while she was settling in to her new life.

"Don't look so sad," Loren said. "I'm not dying. Again. I'll just be here for a little while, to get properly trained as a knight. And then we'll be Nia and Loren, saving the world one artifact at a time again. Only I'll no longer be a sidekick. I'll be a bona fide hero."

I nodded, holding back tears for the second time in two nights. "You are a freakin' heroine."

"Besides, you're leaving me with six hot knights in shining armor. This is heaven."

I laughed. Then I cocked my head to the side, sensing an opportunity. "Listen, since you're now a part of the family and all, they'll probably allow you up on the higher floors."

"Yeah..."

"So, if you happened to have access to the vault where they keep their trove of recovered items..."

"You want me to steal from my newfound family?"

"No, no. Not steal. Just take some pictures. Maybe put something aside for show and tell when I come back."

"OMG, you are relentless."

I stopped, feeling my throat choke up again. "You're gonna be okay."

Loren nodded. I saw her throat working as

though she were trying to swallow a lump. "I'm gonna be okay."

"You're gonna behave?"

She snorted.

I laughed again. Then I pulled her into my arms. I wasn't any gentler this time.

"Oh my god." Loren sniffed. "You're crying."

"I'm not crying; you're crying."

"This isn't forever. Just a small solo tour and then we're getting the band back together."

"Hey," I said as I squeezed. "You're totally gonna women's liberate this place, aren't you?"

"Hell yeah."

"That's my girl."

I left Loren in the bed. Out in the hall, a window of the castle was open. I breathed deep. The salt water from the sea hit my nose as I descended the steps of Tintagel. The bite of the tangy mineral stung the insides of my nose as I inhaled, pulling it down into myself. I straightened my back as I walked the curve of the stairs, not making a misstep. I knew what I had to do.

I had to figure out if Igraine's prophecy was real. If Yod's last words about a sacrifice and a garden were true. There had to be a record, somewhere. And there was only one place I knew to look.

I stopped in a doorway that led into the weapons room and watched the two men as they charged each other. Honey-golden skin met sand-kissed skin as blade met blade. Tres and Gawain sparred in the armory of the castle. The two men were equally matched, and the friendly battle between them ended in a stalemate.

Neither man appeared daunted, their chests heaving and their muscles rippling as they clasped their empty hands together, their sword hands meeting at their chests. Then Tres caught my eye.

He sheathed his sword and made his way over to me. "That blonde tornado doing okay?"

I smiled. "She'll live, so you'd better gird your fortune."

Tres smirked. "What about you?"

"I'll live, too."

"No, I mean, are you doing okay?"

I tried to force a smile, but my lips wouldn't lie. "I think we're in danger."

"From Merlin?"

"Maybe? I don't know."

Tres came closer. He reached out a hand and ran it down the side of my face. "What aren't you telling me, Theta?"

"A lot. But I will tell you. I just need you to come with me."

"Where are we headed?" he asked.

I took a deep breath, and then I said a word I've never said to another living soul. "Home. I need to go home. Will you come with me?"

The adventure continues as Nia goes back to her roots in
Serpent Mound
Book Four of the Nia Rivers Adventures.

But first, check out Loren's first solo adventure in
The Spear of Destiny,
Book One of The Misadventures of Loren!

These two stories happen at the same time and overlap,
so you can read them in either order.

Lover of fairytales, folklore, and mythology, Ines Johnson spends her days reimagining the stories of old in a modern world. She writes books where damsels cause the distress, princesses wield swords, and moms save the world.

You can sign up for her mailing list and receive alerts and free reads at http://bit.ly/InesReaders.

The Nia Rivers Adventures

Dragon Bones

Demeter's Tablet

Templar Scrolls

Serpent Mound

Eden's Garden

The Misadventures of Loren

Spear of Destiny

Ring of Gyges

Hammer of God

www.ingramcontent.com/pod-product-compliance
Lightning Source LLC
Chambersburg PA
CBHW071236190726
48292CB00007B/2319